At Home Among Sinners

AT HOME AMONG SINNERS

A NOVEL
BY
ELIZABETH UPTON

ISBN: 0-9722721-7-8

Cover design by Robert Aulicino

Published by Twin Star, Santa Barbara Press
Santa Barbara, CA 93105
Visit Elizabeth Upton at www.elizabethaupton.com

First paperback edition, 2016

Printed in the United States of America

To my sister Eileen

Other Works by Elizabeth Upton
The Shaman and the Mafia
Secrets of Nun: My Own Story
Exuberant Women Don't Age: No Time to Waste

ACKNOWLEDGEMENTS

Through the years my sister Eileen has supported me, especially in tough times. I am also deeply grateful to my husband Melvin, who believes in me. I am pleased to have Benjamin Swihart as my copy editor and publishing manager.

Dave Bemis has done an outstanding job as my content editor, and given me smart advice. The process of writing novels can take many unexpected turns, and I have been fortunate to have this wonderful team to assist me.

And finally, I appreciate the assistance of Beth Adan and Erica Montgomery of Three Girls Media for their fine publicity work for all of my books to date.

CHAPTER 1

Father John Callahan fumed as the contractor's crew arrived with their tools and heavy equipment. Five rowdy young men smoking, laughing, talking about sex. How dare they defile this hallowed monastery? How could God and the church allow these ancient stones, for so long a holy place of silence and prayer, to become a luxury hotel for the profane and frivolous? He silently cursed the financial ruin that had forced this decision, and which in turn was dispersing the local monks to other monasteries throughout Ireland and Europe.

All of the monks, that is, except for Father John Callahan.

With anger and grief filling his chest to bursting, he waited silently outside the monastery to be taken to the Dublin airport. With him stood Father Jules, the grim-faced abbot who had replaced Father Benedict after his death three months ago. Abbot Jules had decided that Callahan would not go to another monastery, but serve a parish in New York City.

Callahan could hear the wild Irish Sea raging against the rocky cliffs, distraught, it seemed, at the monks' departures. Seagulls flew above the sun, their silver wings glowing as they flapped in the wind. He considered what little he had heard about New York City: crowded, dirty, noisy, profligate. Would he ever return to the lush grass of Ireland's rolling moors and breathe so deeply in its salty air?

"You've been bent on punishing me," he snarled at Father Jules. "You could easily have sent me to another monastery in Ireland."

"That's what you think," growled the abbot. "You came to us, a married man who has tasted to excess the dregs of sin and carnal pleasures, with rumors of a corrupt past, to have a shocking influence on the pure hearts of our young monks. Worse still, you question the Holy Church's doctrines."

"Corrupt past! Listen to me —"

"I'm not finished," Jules nearly shouted as his eyes narrowed. "Abbot Benedict made the unfortunate mistake of allowing you to become a monk before he died, but I dare say you will be at home among the worst of sinners." With that, he walked quickly to the cab that had just arrived, without even the simple courtesy of a wave.

"It's easy to hate the likes of you and to question what you stand for," Callahan shouted, shaking his fist at the departing cab. The abbot's final comment, "You'll be at home among the worst of sinners," burned white-hot in his heart.

* * *

Outside La Guardia airport, in the heart of New York City, Father Callahan sweltered in the August humidity as he stood with the small leather suitcase that held all of his possessions. Still reeling from his first experience with airports and airplanes, he was distraught with the mass of frantic people that now swirled around him. Although a mature man of thirty-three, he felt like an orphan child as he worried about whether the housekeeper at his new parish rectory had forgotten to pick him up.

As the crowd continued to jostle and bump him and his wait reached thirty minutes, he fumbled in his pockets for cab money but found only a few Irish coins. Then a gray Chevy sedan rolled to the curb and a robust, gray-haired, sixtyish woman jumped out.

"Are you Father Callahan?" she asked, breathless.

"I am."

She pushed her hand into his quickly. "I'm Rosemary Waters, the housekeeper at Saint Francis of Assisi rectory. Hop in."

Relieved, he jumped into the car's back seat.

"Sorry about being so late. Never can tell about traffic conditions around New York City."

She sped off, weaving skillfully through traffic. It was close to 7 p.m., and the sun was nearly invisible when they entered the darkening city with its tall gray buildings squeezed cheek to cheek. He looked for flowers, for trees, for tall grass, but saw none. He felt instead the grip of claustrophobia and the terror of chaos.

Cars barely stopped for red lights. Cabs didn't bother, and on street corners old men were pushing rickety shopping carts, miraculously avoiding the onslaught of rushing traffic.

"My God!" he gasped.

"Welcome to New York City," Rosemary said with a smile. "In time all of this will become second nature to you."

As she stole glances at him in her rear view mirror, she continued to be surprised. She had expected to pick up some old, ugly, bent-over monk. Instead Callahan was tall, youthful, athletic — and strikingly handsome — with wavy black hair and penetrating, crystal-blue eyes.

Lost in his own thoughts, Callahan tried to fight off the depression engulfing him. The smell of traffic fumes and city soot pushed through the car's open windows.

"Stop!" he shouted. "There's a man lying at the curb. We must see what's wrong with that poor fellow."

Rosemary sped past. "Not a good idea, Father. He's drunk, drugged or dead," she said casually. "In time the police will gather him up."

"Gather him up? Jesus, help us!"

She drove to Saint Francis of Assisi Church on the city's West Side and into the rectory's garage. Every inch of the rectory and its grounds looked old and worn out.

"Please follow me," she said.

They walked up six stairs to the old kitchen, and she offered him a welcome cup of tea. He remarked that every pot and pan had an organized place.

"I've been the housekeeper here for the past fifteen years, since my husband died, God rest his soul."

"Do you enjoy being a rectory housekeeper?" he asked in an attempt to be cheerful.

"It gives me a steady income," she replied.

"Where is the pastor?"

"He's coming from the church through the breezeway — a wonderful convenience in bad weather."

Rosemary began to put dishes of roast beef, mashed potatoes, steaming gravy and mixed vegetables on the table as they waited for Father Alex to arrive in the small dining room. The bay window's venetian blinds showed their age, some broken at the edges, but they were shiny clean. The worn oak floors glowed with high-gloss polish.

Through the open doorway of the dining room he saw sunken chairs and sofas that looked as if they had not been replaced since the church rectory was built some seventy-five years ago.

"Whom am I replacing?" he asked.

Rosemary managed a tight laugh. "Priests come and go so fast I can't keep track. Usually just been ordained — real green behind the ears."

"There has to be a problem, then?"

"Problem? You'll find out soon enough," she said sourly.

Father Alex entered the dining room. He looked seventy-plus, short, skinny, with a shaven head. Callahan extended a hand.

"I'm Father Callahan," he said.

But the pastor kept his hands and arms stiff as steel at his bony sides. "So they've sent me some dumb monk-priest from Ireland, of all the damned places," he snarled, barely glancing at him.

"At least you have a priest to help out in your parish," Father Callahan replied curtly.

Seated at the table, they ate stonily, without conversation. Father Alex soon began slurping his second glass of wine.

Rosemary kept her eyes on the handsome new priest. He'd be gone in weeks. Too bad, she thought, as she put homemade apple pie on the table with a large dish of vanilla ice cream.

"You're a fine cook," he said appreciatively.

"Such kind words," she replied, and returned to the kitchen. Father Alex had not acknowledged her with so much as a nod. Father Callahan watched him lick drops of wine from his glass, as he ordered a third. It didn't take long for him to realize that the pastor had a problem.

"Why can't Rosemary eat with us instead of eating alone in that hot, stuffy kitchen? It's rather inconsiderate, don't you think?"

Rosemary edged closer to the dining room, listening in amazement at the new priest's bluntness.

"It's not the custom for housekeepers to eat with priests, given our priestly rank . . . ever," he said, pushing his plates aside.

"Our priestly rank?"

"You heard me."

Disgusted, Callahan made no reply.

"Our janitor quit yesterday," Father Alex griped.

"Why?"

"Can't pay him. Not enough money coming into the parish for months. You better get used to doing all of the janitorial work around here. The cleaning materials are in the church basement. Start tomorrow."

As a monk, Father Callahan was used to such work. He held his peace.

"Please show me my room," he said.

"Come with me," Father Alex said, belching loudly and stumbling slightly as he walked to the basement. They came to a windowless room, the air thick with dust and sickening fumes emanating from the oil furnace. Callahan walked carefully, sidestepping the rat droppings that littered the entire concrete floor. He pulled a handkerchief to his nose, his dinner lifting to his throat.

"That's your bed in the corner." It had a thin mattress with no linen, thick with dirt and covered with spider webs.

"Who gives you the right to put me in this rat-infested basement?" Callahan nearly shouted. "Rosemary told me that there are four respectable bedrooms in the rectory, two upstairs and two downstairs."

"This is where you are to stay. Where are your bags?"

"One in the living room."

"There's a small closet in the corner." He turned around, starting up the stairs.

Father Callahan was hot on his heels.

"You're crazy if you think for half a second I will sleep in that rat-infested hole." His voice lifted angrily.

"That's where I intend you to stay."

"Intend doesn't work for me. I'll stay in one of the bedrooms on the first floor that Rosemary mentioned. If you think I'm some dumb, simple-minded monk from Ireland that you can treat like crap, you're out of your mind."

Callahan grabbed his suitcase and went into the first-floor bedroom, slamming the door.

"That turd doesn't belong here," Father Alex said to Rosemary as he staggered into the kitchen. "He's arrogant, belligerent, and he dares to challenge my God-given authority."

Rosemary stared back at him, clearly upset.

"In all due respect, Father Callahan is not some wimpy young priest you can insult and push around like all the rest. He told me he's a widower, went to Oxford, was a high school principal no less, taught science. And he's still only thirty-three. That's impressive, if you ask me."

"I didn't ask you, and I don't give a rat's ass what lies he's told you. I'll get him gone like all the rest."

Father Alex didn't intimidate her. She had worked at Saint Francis since before he was pastor. She prided herself on being a self-sufficient woman making a respectable living.

He wiped his dripping mouth with his cassock sleeve and weaved to the second floor, pausing and gripping the banister. She called after him. "It's in your best interest to treat Father Callahan with respect."

* * *

Father Callahan began to calm in spurts, grateful that his room had a shower and a tub, and a window that looked out on a patch of sky peeking past a tall gray building. But he wondered how long he could put up with the pastor's abusive attitude.

In the kitchen, as Rosemary finished her work for the evening, she laughed out loud. She had no doubt in her mind that Father Alex had met his match at last.

CHAPTER 2

As she watched him from across the street, Sheila leaned against the front of a hat shop, eating corn chips and then dropping the bag carelessly onto the gum-stained New York City sidewalk. She often passed the old church on the way to her apartment's shady business in Midtown.

This new man was a looker, no doubt about it, slender and fit, his shirtsleeves rolled high. He labored hard to scrub filth from the six-foot statue of Saint Francis of Assisi in front of the church. The run-down gothic building's bronze bells tolled electronically on the hour of twelve.

She continued to study the man's striking features, licking the tips of her fingers and enjoying the taste of sea salt. She was rapt in fascination with the way he brushed off layers of bug-crusted dirt from the statue, next taking a wet towel to wipe with great care the statue's small bronze dove and gray wolf that lay snuggling at its base. He must be the church's new janitor, she thought, an appealing change from the homely former church workers who'd been older than Einstein.

"You'd think he was preparing that old statue for an exhibit at the Metropolitan Museum, the way he's tending to it," she thought. Then she heard him start to sing in a thrilling baritone the Irish pop song "All Kinds of Everything." The tender lyrics touched her heart. Perhaps this young janitor was thinking of someone he loved, and it gave him comfort to sing such a sweet love song.

Observing him soothed her for some unknown reason. She watched him finish his work, pick up his ladder and two tin pails, and enter the church. She tossed the rest of her lunch onto the curb and crossed the street, the wind lifting her loose short skirt.

A young man whistled as he drove close to her in his Jaguar, enjoying her long, naked legs and the low-cut blouse that revealed an exciting bosom. "Hey, baby, want a lift?" he called. She laughed and playfully gave him the finger, swinging her hips as she entered the church.

For a few seconds she hesitated, then slowly opened one of the ten-foot-high oak doors and crept into the church. The heavy scent of burning candles and frankincense swept her back to age seven, the year her family had stopped attending Mass altogether.

She saw the janitor in front of the altar, and he was changing from his work clothes into a long black cassock. Then he opened the door of the confessional, turning on the outside light — announcing he was ready to hear confessions.

"Surprise, surprise!" she stage-whispered, loud enough to be heard. She took note of Father John Callahan's name etched on a thin wooden panel outside the confessional door.

She looked around casually at the large statues nestled cozily in the corners of the church hall, their ivory halos aglow from the sunlight that streamed through tall stained-glass windows. They seemed so real. As a child she had imagined them engrossed in lively conversation.

But now her adoration for the mysteries of God was long gone. A stirring of sadness overcame her—sadness for lost innocence, and the loss of the comfort that had once come with faith in what could not be seen. *Leave now*, she cautioned herself. *Stay*, another voice taunted. Each thought battled the other, wreaking havoc in her head.

* * *

Father Callahan had seen the young woman wearing a scarlet see-through blouse as she had watched him from across the street. He had known her kind well since he was a boy growing up in Ireland. A house of prostitution three blocks from his high school had seduced lustful teenage boys, who'd save their money, fall in love, and have their hearts broken. He remembered when the women often sang, "No money, honey, no lovin' tonight." He stifled a laugh at the memory.

It was easy to watch her from inside the confessional, as she moved about touching the gilt edges of the Stations of the Cross that were engraved deep in plastered walls. She appeared conflicted. Perhaps she didn't want to be here. If that was the case, it made two of them.

The musty smell inside the warm confessional was far from inviting. The woman coughed, nervously pulling back the heavy purple drape to kneel on a hard oak kneeler that seemed intended to urge penitents to confess their sins and leave quickly.

Christ, whatever she says, make it fast, he prayed, loosening the top buttons on his cassock.

"I don't know how to begin," she said. "Actually, I don't want to be here. I just need someone to confide in." She inhaled deeply, lifting the low-cut blouse that barely covered her breasts, which were easy to see through the thin curtain that separated her from the priest.

Confessors were instructed to keep their heads down and not look at their penitents. He regarded this as silly rule, and had no compunction ignoring it.

"I haven't been in church since I made my first communion," she began haltingly.

"A stretch of time, I'd say."

"I'm twenty-six," she announced in an edgy, high-pitched voice. "Guess it's kinda long."

"Whisper, lassie, if you don't want New York City to hear what you dearly want kept secret."

She half laughed. But her unbearably long pause got to him.

"Please tell me what's on your mind."

"I feel you'll admonish me."

"Well, lassie, lay it out. Let's see if I'll be so inclined."

She giggled nervously.

"I'm in love."

"Good for you. Love is a wondrous thing."

"But . . . but . . . the man I love is very married."

"It happens," he said, with no trace of reproach.

"It wasn't supposed to happen. Awful for my lifestyle and business."

"Care to spell it out?" he said. He had a strong idea of what that might be.

"I am a well-paid call girl. I service men in high places who pay me a ton of money to get them off — if you know what I mean." She waited.

"Continue, please," he replied, tempted to laugh.

"I should have broken off serving him. Trouble is, I didn't. Every day he tells me how much he's in love with me — swears to God he's going to divorce his wife."

"Has he left his wife yet?"

"Going to. Keeps promising."

"Of course not. A smart woman in your trade should know how it works."

"What the hell do you know about my trade?" she hissed, bristling.

"I'm not naïve. I've been a man in the world," he replied. He heard her swear under her breath. "Are you here to receive counsel? If not, best you leave this confessional," he said, his voice rising.

"You have a temper," she retorted.

"Call it what you may, but don't waste my time. If I can help you, I'll do so." With a great deal of effort, he softened his tone.

She paused a beat. "I'm sorry," she whispered contritely.

"Please continue," he replied gently.

"Glenn Hudson, the man I'm in love with, is the New York State attorney general," she said, gulping. "He has three young kids, and a savvy, rich, socialite wife."

He leaned forward in his chair. "Did I hear you correctly? This man is the attorney general for New York State?"

She sniffled. "Yes, and he goes to church every freaking Sunday with his family," she said, beginning to weep.

"Do you want my advice or are you here just to talk?"

"Maybe both, but right now Glenn will be waiting impatiently for our love time. He's always early, and can't wait for what I do for him." She rose, pulling back the drape to leave the confessional. Father Callahan stepped out and moved in front of her.

"I'm here to help . . . if that's what you really want?" he offered sincerely.

"I'll be back," she promised, wiping her eyes with an embroidered cotton handkerchief from her Chanel purse. She glanced at her Rolex.

This woman was living high on the hog, he observed. He wondered what else she might be into.

"By the way, where did you get your lunch?"

"How do you know about my lunch?"

"Years past I was a high school teacher, and rarely failed to notice what was going on with the kids no matter where they were. Served me well then."

She decided then she rather liked him. At least he wasn't a pious, wimpy priest. *Maybe he's what I honestly need*, she mused.

"Go down two blocks and on the left corner you'll come to Tony's Deli. Do you like corned beef sandwiches?"

"My favorite."

"Then you're in for a treat."

"By the way lassie, how about picking up that lunch bag you tossed on the sidewalk and put it in a trashcan?"

She made no response. *No surprise there*, he thought.

"My name is Sheila," she said, smiling, her pretty dimples deepening. She swept red polished fingernails through her waist-length blond hair. He had no trouble acknowledging that she was a young beauty, and she knew it.

"Take care," he said with a light Irish lilt, and went into the sacristy to change into his street clothes, black pants and black shirt. He wondered if Sheila would have it in her to return. The fact she told him he had a temper didn't upset him in the least.

* * *

Sheila thought about Father Callahan. Every inch of him shouted that he had had plenty of experience with women. She began to wonder how he would be as a lover. After all, it was her business to make such assessments.

* * *

Thinking of Glenn Hudson, the attorney general of New York, left a foul taste in his mouth as he strolled to Tony's Deli through heavy waves of humidity.

He saw Sheila prance across the street like a pampered poodle, kicking her lunch bag close to the gutter, then stooping to toss it into the trash can. She proceeded to strut down the sidewalk, advertising the fact that she wore no panties.

A sleek black Porsche drove to the curb, and a man's long arm pushed open the car door. She hopped into the front seat and spread her feet wide on the dashboard. The man's hand slid down her legs.

"Hey, don't get into that car," Callahan yelled. Holy Mother of God! Was this driver a customer, a stranger, or a predator?

CHAPTER 3

He finished his corned beef sandwich only because he hated wasting food. In his foul mood, it tasted like cardboard. He blamed Sheila for his miserable state of mind, and he tried to brush aside her actions as well as her depressing revelations.

As a confessor, he was exhorted to listen passively and compassionately, without condemnation, to people's life struggles and sins. But this cockroach Glenn Hudson, New York State's attorney general and a degenerate, flaming phony, make his stomach turn.

After lunch he knelt before the altar, yearning for the solitude of Ireland's serene monastery, praying for the delusional Sheila's welfare. In vain he tried to rid his vision of her in the Porsche and struggled with thoughts of how he could help. Was the passive, non-judgmental listening of a confessor the best he could offer her? Or anyone, for that matter?

On the way to the rectory he paused and looked out back at a neglected greenhouse with four-foot weeds winding around it. Curious, he began to investigate the decrepit structure that he assumed had once been beautiful.

He couldn't see through the windows in the greenhouse because of their crust of dirt and cobwebs. A large rusty padlock made the door impossible to open, so he turned and walked into the rectory.

When he entered the dining room Rosemary was ironing linen altar cloths, steam floating lazily above her head. He sat near her.

"I rarely see Father Alex. What does he do all day?" he asked. "He just says one Sunday Mass, nothing much in the church bulletins . . . haven't even seen him in the rectory office."

"You're right. He's not around. Drinks and watches soap operas all day," she said, shaking her head in disgust.

"Amazing he's still a pastor," Callahan said. He decided to let the issue rest as he admired the skill in which Rosemary ironed the stiff, starched church linens. "I thought church volunteers did the altar ironing," he said.

"It's been years since the altar society's done the ironing, thanks to Father Alex. The parish has gone to rot since he's been pastor." She made no effort to hide her annoyance.

"I'd rather enjoy helping you. We monks did everything in the monastery — ironing, cooking, shopping, and cleaning. I loved caring for our farm animals, and I did it every day because the other monks dreaded the task."

Rosemary lifted her head, surprised. "What do you miss the most?" She pulled the iron's plug out of the wall and wiped her face from the steam.

He rocked back in his chair, closing his eyes.

"I miss the peacefulness, the land, the moors, holy prayers, silence — and those precious animals." When he mentioned the animals, his voice lowered, showing evidence of melancholy.

"I suspect you must have had a favorite animal?" she probed, sitting beside him.

"Ah, yes, that was Noble, a fiery white stallion with a bigger-than-life attitude," he said poetically. "I'd ride him through the moors with Max, our sheep dog, racing beside us. Together we'd gallop free and wild up and down the moors with the smell of the Irish Sea caressing us." For more than a while they sat in silence as vaults of hidden memories opened and swept through him.

* * *

In his teens he had often seen her at the edge of the rolling moors, watching him gallop his horse bareback, often shirtless in the early morning. As the sun began to warm the dewy grass, he'd hear her calling.

"Come to me, laddie," she'd call, but he'd ride on, ignoring the lustful longing in her young voice. So many times he'd heard that voice while riding in the early morning.

One day she was out much earlier, waiting. When he drew near she ripped off her blouse, jumping gleefully into the air and running after him. "Come to me, handsome lad!" she called.

He swung his horse toward her. "Lassie, do you know what you're wanting?" he laughed huskily, aroused to fullness by her exciting young body.

"Oh, I do," she begged. "Just one kiss," licking her rosy lips.

"Aye, Lassie, 'tis more than a kiss you want from me."

"Just one kiss," she begged, her pretty face flushed with desire. She tugged on his pant leg.

"One kiss it will be," he said, sliding off his horse and dropping the reins. Her lips were soft and warm when she pressed her luscious breasts against his naked chest. In seconds he laid her deep in the willowy grass. No words were spoken until the sun had risen far beyond the moors.

"I must be gone, sweet love," he said, swinging his hips high onto his horse as it pawed the soft ground. "Your father will kill me if he finds out what we've done."

"I'm of age," she pouted.

"Aye, lassie, it won't much matter. Wait no more for me," he cautioned.

"I love you!" she shouted.

"You don't know what love is, nor I. Forget me." He galloped away, still hard with lust, knowing it would be the last time he'd lie with her.

"I won't forget you," she called, her tender voice echoing through the rising mist. For the briefest of moments he spun around to savor the freshness of her beauty, no longer innocent.

He inhaled deeply, allowing the memories of those young wild days to fade away, but their ache refused to leave.

* * *

Rosemary wondered how long he'd last before he'd had his fill of Father Alex.

"What happened to the animals when the monastery closed?" she asked, curious to know more about him.

"A kind farmer took all of them. He promised I could have Noble any time, but that's an impossible dream," he said, shading his eyes with his hand to keep her from seeing the full extent of his feelings.

She placed two steaming cups of tea along with honey-glazed donuts on the table. They were unaware that Father Alex had been sitting out of sight near the top of the staircase, listening to their conversation with owl-like concentration.

"I wonder why the greenhouse remains in such disrepair?" Father Callahan mused.

"You must forget the greenhouse." She rose, shaking. "Father Alex hates it with a passion that frightens me."

"Forgive me if I have upset you. I do not mean to trouble you, but I am thinking how wondrous it would be to have it restored for church flowers, and flowers for the sick and homebound," Father Callahan said.

She sat down heavily, pulling her rosary beads from her apron pocket and thumbing them feverishly.

"Years ago the greenhouse was a glorious place for flowers, thanks to the generosity of the McBride family."

"It must have been," he said soothingly.

She gave a small nod, working her beads through sweaty fingers.

"The greenhouse provided hundreds of flowers for weddings, special events, funerals, with dozens of generous volunteers. But since his arrival, Father Alex has forbidden its use. The one time I tried to enter, I feared he might hurt me. I've never seen him so angry."

He opened a kitchen drawer that was filled with nails, assorted tools and a host of odds and ends, taking out a large hammer.

"I feel evil and harm will come to me for revealing all this."

"You have nothing to be fear," he said confidently. Emotionally exhausted, Rosemary wiped her moist eyes with a tiny handkerchief and fell quiet.

Father Alex stumbled halfway down the staircase, shouting, "In the name of God, I forbid you to enter the greenhouse!" He held tight to the banister with his right hand, and to his shaking wine glass with his left.

"It has be done," Father Callahan answered, upset that Alex had been listening to their private conversation. "The greenhouse can be a gift from God for the good of this parish."

"On my authority as pastor of this church, I forbid you to enter the greenhouse," he yelled, pounding on the banister. Ignoring his tirade, Father Callahan turned and walked away. "You will be cursed.

You will be damned to Hell!" He shouted, even more loudly, then weaved unsteadily to his room.

Rosemary's hands shook slightly as she gathered her basket of linens. Contemplating what Alex might do next disturbed her deeply. Nonetheless, a heavy burden had been lifted from her heart. She beseeched God to keep Father Callahan safe from the onslaught of Father Alex's blasphemous curse.

* * *

Callahan pushed through thick weeds to the greenhouse door, hammer in hand. He slammed the old padlock until it shattered and he could open the door. Rats scurried to find safer places to hide. He grasped a filthy broom and swept aside sticky cobwebs.

The greenhouse was desolate and empty, and he nearly gagged in the foul air. As he stepped into the sunshine he coughed until he doubled over.

"Hey, you okay?" a strong voice called from behind him. He turned, looking into the concerned face of a pleasant-looking, fiftyish man close to his height.

"Maybe too much lunch," Callahan said.

"I'm looking for a priest around here."

"I'm Father Callahan."

"I'm Detective Ronald Casey. Like to talk to you."

Father Callahan leaned against the wrought iron gate, trying to control his breathing. Casey glanced at his car parked in a red zone in front of the rectory.

"Give me a sec . . . I think I'm being paged." He ran to his car and then shouted, "Sorry, Padre, gotta leave. Catch you tomorrow. I need to talk to you." He drove away into the thick of traffic.

CHAPTER 4

Why did some cop want to speak to me? Father Callahan wondered. He had enough to deal with. He lit a seven-day candle in front of the statue of Saint Michael the archangel.

"Help me restore this greenhouse treasure," he prayed, "and deliver me from the deranged curse of Father Alex."

He moved back and forth restlessly in the front pew. He flipped off his sandals and stretched his long legs. Why couldn't he at least restore the greenhouse to what it had been, and clean up the rectory's sickening, infested backyard?

He strode through the church breezeway to the rectory and found Rosemary stirring a pot of beef stew. Its delicious aroma lifted his mood.

She glanced at him, resolved not to ask about the greenhouse. No good would come of it, she convinced herself. He leaned against the kitchen door, taking a moment to gather his thoughts.

"The greenhouse's yard is despicable. Know of any gardeners up for the job?"

"It's been a sorry sight for years," she said, taking her address book from her purse. She flipped through worn pages and wrote down a name. She returned to the stove.

After a few minutes Father Callahan announced, "I've been able to get the Adams Landscape and Pest Control Company. A man named Harold says to expect them within the hour. The backyard is infested with rats, and every species of bug, as is our filthy rectory basement." He sat at the dining room table sipping a steamy cup of tea and buttering a slice of corn bread, dipping it into a bowl of beef stew.

"Please don't take me wrong," she said anxiously, "but you must watch your step with Father Alex. He'll throw a fit with you taking over like this."

"Frankly, I don't care. He lives in his bottle, neglects his pastoral responsibilities. I have no respect for the likes of him."

Rosemary's lips widened ever so slightly.

"I was thinking you'd know of a holy monastery in these parts," he said in an abrupt change of topic.

"Holy? I'd think they are all holy."

"Of course, but is there one you've heard is exceptional?"

"Um . . . one does come to mind," she said, brightening, "but it's not Catholic. A monastery in the Catskills, I've heard mentioned, but it's ... Buddhist of some sort. Folks rave about a monk living there, with a peculiar name . . . Thron . . . yes, that's it, Monk Thron."

"I miss the monastery," he said, longing for the peace and silence he had known until so recently. "I'll take the parish car and drive up to that one," he said.

Rosemary shook her head vehemently. "You don't have a New York State driver's license."

"It shouldn't be a problem. I've driven for years in Ireland."

"Father Alex won't allow you to take the parish car." Her left eye twitched.

"Does our virtuous Father Alex have a driver's license?"

She threw her hands in the air, laughing.

"He lost it with more DUIs than I can count. Besides, he has cataracts."

"We don't have to tell him," he insisted.

"How about if I drive you up there?"

But he wanted to be free to do whatever he pleased, even though he was uncertain what that might be.

"I might want to stay overnight," he said, refusing to be put off.

"Then you're gonna have to get a temporary driver's license. Cops patrol that neck of woods like vultures. I've been pulled over just for blowing my nose. Why not visit some Catholic monastery around here? It would be less trouble for sure."

"Truth is, I'm now rather eager to meet this Monk Thron," he said.

* * *

In an hour a gardening crew arrived, and two pest control workers put on masks and entered the rectory basement. The gardeners set about methodically removing densely overgrown weeds, piles of stones, and smelly trash from the backyard. The pest controllers killed dozens of scurrying rats, putting them in trash bags and setting dozens more traps. They made preparations to return each day for the rest of the week.

Harold, the burly foreman who looked more like a bouncer than an exterminator, directed his men to wash the exterior of the greenhouse and all of the grounds.

"Want the inside of the greenhouse hosed down?" he asked.

"Clear the whole place out from top to bottom," Callahan directed, knotting his arms behind his back.

He kept his distance while he watched the men work. They filled wheelbarrows with the decayed flowerpots and hauled broken wood to Dumpsters hooked to the back of their trucks. Then they hosed the inside structure from top to bottom, leaving the greenhouse looking immaculate for the first time in many years.

* * *

Rosemary drove him to the DMV, pointing out the corner bus stop so he could get home. The old DMV's ash-gray building was jammed with irritated people, waiting in long, winding lines. Preoccupied mothers ignored their shrieking children, who were running up and down the grimy floors. No one chatted. No one smiled. Most simply waited, stoic but angry.

Forty minutes passed before the middle-aged, bleach-blond clerk waved him to her counter. She spoke with a lit cigarette dangling from lips to which lipstick had been pasted with far too heavy a hand. She barely glanced at him.

"I need a driver's license today," Father Callahan said, which told her he must be newly arrived from Mars.

"Mister Callahan, you'll get a temp license in four weeks," she said, coughing hoarsely in his face.

"Excuse me, Madam, but as I said, I absolutely need a license today."

She laughed, her voice deep and raspy from heavy smoking.

"Madam?"

Her next words caught him by surprise. "Well, well, that's a first. Show me your previous driver's license." He fumbled through his wallet and handed it to her.

"From Ireland! Damn! Invalid."

"Got a birth certificate?" For a brief moment she took note of the frustration covering his striking features, and softened as much as her New York City attitude allowed. "How old are you?"

"Thirty-three."

"You look like a boy to me."

He grinned, but wasn't flattered.

"You must believe me. I'm an excellent driver."

"I bet you are, driving up the hills and dales of Ireland," she said, snickering loudly. "Gotta know, mister, you're in the Big Apple now. Real different here."

She scratched a date on a thin piece of paper. "Come back next week. Bring in your birth certificate. Prepare to take a road and written test next Thursday. Usually takes four weeks, but anyone calling me Madam deserves a break," she said with a broad wink.

Then in a scratchy voice she shouted, "Next!"

Father Callahan thought that, at this rate, meeting Monk Thron would take an eternity. Since he had arrived at Saint Francis of Assisi, there had been nothing to offer him a shard of comfort. He couldn't even restore the greenhouse without Father Alex's vindictive curse hanging over him.

CHAPTER 5

He walked up and down the church aisles, seeking peace of mind after his frustrating encounter at the DMV. As he was about to open his breviary, a little book of liturgical texts, and pray the psalms he heard strange sounds coming from back of the church. He slid out of his pew, looking around, and saw no one.

God help me, he thought. He grabbed a processional cross, a long silver pole with a metal cross mounted on top, and walked heavily down the aisle, pausing from time to time to look around and listen.

Jesus! The sounds were coming from his confessional. Sucking in a deep breath, he grasped the crucifix pole tighter and kicked the door open, prepared to shout, "Be gone, Satan!"

On the confessional floor was a trembling puppy in a pink wicker basket, standing on its small hind legs, peering into his face with sad brown eyes. Father Callahan picked up the pup snugly in his arms, and she began licking him from ear to ear. On the floor were a soft rose-colored blanket and a letter. When he ripped it open, tags fell out, identifying the puppy as "Woofy," with a New York City license.

Dear Father,

Woofy is a spayed female, six months young, fifteen pounds—a pedigree mutt, has all her shots, no fleas, in good health, loveable, potty trained, and smart as a whip. I know she'll love you. Please care for her. I am too ill to do that, and it gives me comfort to know Woofy will have a loving friend.

He sighed. "Little pup, it feels like I need you as much as you need me." He carried his new charge tenderly to the rectory. Woofy had the pointed ears of a collie and was entirely black except for her long tan legs. Her shiny coat smelled of fresh lavender. He carried her toys, blanket and the two cans of dog food he had found in the basket to the kitchen where Rosemary was rolling slabs of dough for the supper's apple pie.

"I have a new little friend," he said, his face flushed with happiness. He set Woofy down on the kitchen floor and she immediately set off to explore. "You must read this letter," he said, pushing it into her hands. She watched the pup uneasily and shook her head nervously as she put on her reading glasses.

"I swear to God, Father Alex will go nuts with that dog running about. What's her name again?"

"Woofy." At the sound of her name, the pup cocked her head and barked in a high, squeaky voice.

"She'll fit in just fine," he said, ignoring Rosemary's eyebrows, which had lifted to her hairline.

Sure enough, Father Alex came out of the first-floor office to glare at him and the puppy. "Get rid of that . . . that horrid creature," he slurred.

"A dying woman has placed her in my protection," Father Callahan answered stiffly.

"You be damned. Get rid of that mongrel by tomorrow or mark my words, if you don't, I will."

Callahan took Woofy gently to his room, shutting his door. "No he won't, little friend," he said, rubbing her soft warm tummy. She looked adoringly into his face, as if she understood every precious word he had promised.

* * *

The woman had squeezed herself behind the baptismal font, sitting on the floor, watching the young priest kissing her little puppy and securing her tight in his arms. It warmed her heart to know that Woofy would be safe.

In vain she tried to lift herself off the floor but her legs proved too weak. "Please, help me," she called to a man who had just entered the church.

"No problem," the man said, lifting her up gently. "Do you need assistance getting home?"

"I'll be fine," she responded.

"I'm Ronald Casey," the man offered.

The woman noticed his police badge tucked inside his jacket and thanked him for his assistance.

"Happen to have seen a young priest around here?"

"Yes. He should be back soon. Confessions begin any moment now." She left the church relieved and happy.

Although Casey had been a lapsed Catholic for decades, he considered himself above reproach compared to the many two-faced jerks who would go to church on Sundays but waltz with the devil for the rest of the week. He had a good feeling about Father Callahan even though their initial exchange had been so brief.

After Callahan had made Woofy comfortable in his bedroom and shut the door behind him, he entered the confessional. So did Casey.

"Bless me, Father," Casey began, surprised he remembered how to bless himself, putting the fingers of his right hand to his forehead, then to his heart, and to his left, then right, shoulder. "Frankly Father, I don't regard myself as an out-and-out sinner."

"Well, lucky you. Since I've been in this godforsaken city, I've longed to meet a sinless man."

Casey was taken aback but he chuckled lightly, his mood improving.

Father Callahan shook his decrepit watch—long in need of replacing. "How may I help you?"

"I believe in the seal of confession," Casey announced.

"And if that is what you need, that's a good thing."

"I notice you have a Irish accent," Casey remarked.

"I lived all of my years in Ireland. Are you also Irish?"

"Both on my grandparents and parents side, born and raised in Derry, Ireland."

"A fine place indeed. Tell me now, what's on your mind?"

Casey cleared his throat, which had grown dry. "Recently I've been reinstated as an NYPD police detective." Father Callahan leaned forward in his hard pine chair, ignoring the stuffiness in the windowless confessional.

"Since my retirement I've had the time of my life traveling throughout Europe. Get this, I had gotten tickets to the Caribbean islands when NYPD Chief Thomas Duffy paid me a visit at my house in Queens and pressured me to work undercover on a serial murder case."

They both heard banging in the back of the church. Casey pulled back his confessional drape, seeing a boy who looked no older than fifteen trying to jam open the collection box. He sprang down the aisle and snatched the kid, shaking him like rocks in a tin can.

"Stealing in church?" he roared, punching the kid in the gut. Built like a broomstick, the teen doubled over and gasped for breath, dropping the coin box.

"Shame on you, stealing money from the poor!" Casey held the boy, twisting him by the scuff of his neck.

"Up yours!" the teen shouted angrily, until he saw Casey's badge and gun. He immediately fell silent, then started to whimper. Tears formed on his cheek.

"So . . . we have a wimp on our hands. I have a mind to drag your sorry ass to jail."

The kid turned the color of paste, unable to utter a syllable.

"I'll pardon you only if you promise not to return and steal," Father Callahan barked.

"I promise . . . promise!" the boy sputtered. Casey shook him again for good measure, then released him.

They watched him run like a greyhound down the street.

"That kid has talent, could be on a track team," Father Callahan remarked. They broke into a fit of laughter as they returned inside the church.

"Let's go to the front sacristy. It's much cooler, and also private."

"That'll do." Casey followed to a small room to the side of the altar and sat on a soft brown, cushioned armchair. A large painting of Saint Francis of Assisi on the wall appeared so real he felt the saint could actually sit with them and join their conversation.

Father Callahan drew a chair in front of him.

Casey reassured himself he wasn't about to make a mistake by confiding in the priest. Over the years he'd learned to wear distrust the way he wore his police vest, thick and hard.

"Chief Duffy gave me the task of finding the serial killer who has murdered two police chiefs' daughters, one in Syracuse and more recently one in Yonkers. It's ridiculous that our police task force, FBI included, has been clueless in finding the fuck. Pardon my French."

"I'm not here to correct your expletives," Callahan said.

"That's a good thing, Padre. Otherwise I'd be a mute." Casey ran his fingers through his thick brown hair. "Chief Duffy forbids me to work at police headquarters. Damn, he delivers all case information to my house."

"Is that a problem?"

"Problem!? Damn. I've been walking through murky catacombs, for shit's sake. I don't even have a lowly creature to brainstorm with. Jeez! Now I'm back to wearing a badge, packing a gun, and driving an unmarked police car. I was supposed to be in the Bahamas by now, tanning, surfing, drinking . . . enjoying women who are panting for my hot body."

"Apparently Chief Duffy has a lot of trust in you."

"Yeah, he's desperate," Casey said, pulling out a cigarette, then suddenly remembering where he was. He quickly stuffed it back into his jacket pocket.

There was nothing soft about this tough, scar-faced, muscled cop, yet he seemed desperate for help.

"I want to support you in any way I can," Callahan offered, and suddenly regretted it, aware it was a thin offer at best. Casey took his time arranging the order of his thoughts, what to expose and what to hold back.

"Eleven months ago, the eighteen-year-old daughter of Police Chief James Knott in Syracuse was raped and strangled in her apartment. The killer used latex gloves and a condom, and left no traceable evidence . . . even wore latex shoe covers. This case is colder than an iceberg, even with the FBI sniffing like bloodhounds."

"How can that be possible?"

"We keep asking that same question," Casey said, rubbing deep worry creases on his forehead. "Three months ago there was another rape and strangulation of Yonkers Police Chief Donald Garrison's nineteen-year-old daughter in her apartment, with the same damn MO.

"I had retired from the police force before any of these murders took place. The second victim's dad had installed a top-grade security system the previous week, but this maniac slithered in like a cobra."

"I can't begin to imagine the suffering of their families," Callahan said, loosening the bottoms of his cassock sleeves.

"I am positive this assassin has a hate-revenge motive for murdering police chiefs' daughters. Each of them is petite, pretty, young . . . raped and murdered in their homes in quiet neighborhoods."

They sat a moment in silence while the church bells tolled mournfully, as if in response to Casey's horrific revelations.

"I've been wondering why the chief called you back, given your retirement, and under all this secrecy."

Casey scraped his shoes back and forth on the floor, sitting upright and uptight.

"In my day I was one of the best. Besides, we've been friends for years. The force will always be my family." He rubbed moisture from his eyes. "I'm telling you flat out, this killer is a hardcore professional, maybe ex-military. He kills and hides until he murders again. Insane."

"But why all this secrecy, insisting you work alone like a hermit?"

"Duffy's convinced he has dirty cops in his vice division, and in the Department of Internal Affairs."

"Any proof?"

"How the hell would I know?" Casey rose from the armchair.

"Allow me to offer you my blessing?"

Casey's knees hit the floor; he was grateful for any crumb to calm his frustration.

"I wonder if you'd be up to doing me a slight favor," the priest asked tentatively.

"Try me," Casey grinned.

"I have to take a driver's test. I've never driven in this city, and always on the right side of a car in Ireland. Perhaps a quick drive around the block will do it?"

"Believe me, Padre, it's going to take more than a quick romp around a New York City block," Casey said with a snicker. "Jump into my car."

Casey sat in the front passenger seat, leaning back as Father Callahan tried to move into the city traffic, barely missing a passing bus. He jerked to a stop when a pedestrian with her head down almost walked into the car, ignoring the light. A cabby blasted his horn, giving him the finger to get moving. At the end of twenty terrifying minutes, Callahan's heart was pounding and sweat was dripping down his back.

"Not too bad," Casey said reassuringly. "A few more city outings will do the trick."

"What a hellish experience," Callahan replied.

"Worry not, Padre. In time driving about in the city will be like a gentle jog in the park. See you soon."

Back outside the car, Callahan watched Casey swing effortlessly into a maze of traffic, his left hand barely on the wheel, while casually lighting a cigarette.

He worried about Casey's search for the serial killer. Before entering the church he leaned against the statue of Saint Francis of Assisi and heaved a sigh.

"We have so much in common," he said out loud to the statue, as if it were alive. "You were once rich, godless, carousing with women, and living a careless life." He ran his fingers reflectively over the saint's bronze heart. "But you were converted from your wayward life, worked miracles, loved humanity and all of its creatures large and small. If only I could be like you."

He glanced at his watch, late for dinner. He hurried to the rectory where he saw only one table setting. "Where is Father Alex?" he asked.

"A drinking friend picked him up for the evening," she said, disgusted, placing a large bowl of vegetables and roast chicken by his plate.

"How about joining me?" he offered pleasantly. She took off her apron and put another setting on the table and sat across from him. "A wonderful first," she gushed.

"It looks like we shall be having a lot of firsts," he said, enjoying her company and her happiness while Woofy chewed contentedly on his shoelaces.

His mind drifted unwillingly to the greenhouse, and then to Casey's murder investigations, and to Sheila's crazy illusions about New York State's attorney general. His performance as a confessor must improve, he tried to convince himself. Suddenly it dawned on him that he wasn't the only one indulging in fantasies.

CHAPTER 6

During the night, heavy rain and early frost freshened the sooty city. He opened the front doors of the church, inhaling the clean air and shivering from this early September's unseasonable cold. At the far left corner outside the church he saw a man wrapped tight in a brown Army blanket. He reminded himself that, but for the grace of God, he could be that man, and decided to let him be.

Father Alex — who was rarely up before ten in the morning — came out of the church's front door and lunged toward the sleeping man, his foot raised and ready to kick him. Father Callahan grabbed his arm, wrestling him away.

"Druggies and bums, the scourge of the earth," Alex hissed angrily, "an abomination on these holy grounds." He struggled himself free from Callahan's grip.

"God Almighty. Get hold of yourself," Father Callahan said, mortified by the pastor's despicable behavior. Father Alex shouted back at him. Callahan pushed him away. "Have you forgotten Jesus' exhortation that we must not judge and must be merciful?"

Father Alex shook his bony fists in Callahan's face, shouting, "Who gives you the right to preach to me, scum?" and fled to the rectory, kicking the sides of the pews as he went down the aisle.

The homeless man had been fully awake and prepared to defend himself. Before the young priest entered the church, he had heard him pray kindly, "May the Lord of love and compassion help and protect you."

The man rose quickly from the cold concrete and folded his blankets neatly, squeezing them in to a large duffle bag. His stomach ached from hunger. He hated picking through the city Dumpsters filled with flies, bugs, and beady-eyed rats. The stench often made him vomit his guts out.

He opened the church door, anxious but relieved that the mean old priest was nowhere to be seen. He closed his eyes, remembering his innocence as an altar boy long ago.

The man's eyes drifted to the kind priest who was now standing in front of the altar. The father's chanted prayers resounded blissfully through the church. The man yearned for comfort and for acceptance . . . but not for salvation. He bent over, rubbing his swollen ankles, aching from the miles he had walked through crowded streets, where people treated him worse than fleas.

The man was in desperate need, and he closed his eyes to savor the warmth and peacefulness of the old church, which seemed strangely foreign.

"Young lad, may I help you?" Father Callahan asked, peering down at him with concern.

He choked up. "I'm desperately hungry. I despise begging and eating from vermin-infested garbage cans. I'll work hard for food. I'm no bum."

Father Callahan reached his hand toward him.

"I'm Father Callahan."

"Derrick," he said, grateful for the kindness of a simple handshake. Callahan was surprised how tidy Derrick was. His clothes, while ragged, were remarkably clean, rare for anyone living on the streets.

"Please come with me," Father Callahan offered. Derrick followed him meekly to the rectory dining room where Rosemary had prepared a hearty breakfast of French toast, eggs, bacon, sausage and a large bowl of fruit, all set on the table around a vase of yellow daisies.

"We have a visitor for breakfast," Callahan announced cheerfully. Rosemary placed another set of dishes on the table. It had been years since anyone other than priests had been invited for a meal, and it lifted her spirits.

"Have a seat," Father Callahan said, indicating the chair next to him. Derrick sat stiffly, worried that if he pissed off the priest, he would throw his ass out. He forced himself not to shovel his food, savoring the steaming cup of coffee that he filled high with sugar and cream.

From the top of the staircase Father Alex watched, unseen again. Furious. How dare that reprobate Callahan feed a tramp in his rectory?

He muttered obscenities beneath his breath, as he fixated on ways to get rid of the upstart priest. A sick plan soon began to simmer in his mind, bringing a smile to his face.

Derrick gulped his food down as if it would soon vanish into thin air.

"Take your time, laddie," Callahan said. "Enjoy your breakfast."

"Used to be Catholic," Derrick mumbled, wiping crumbs from the side of his mouth with the linen napkin.

Father Callahan mused how much he had recently been hearing people say they "used to be" this or that. It was starting to sound like a broken record.

"Where are you from?" he asked.

"Chicago, then drafted in the Vietnam War," he said. "In New York since my discharge."

"I understand it was a terrible war."

"Worse than terrible," the man said. He rubbed his eyes. Rosemary cleared off the dining table.

"I can prepare you a lunch," Rosemary offered their guest.

"We can do much better than that," Father Callahan said, leaving the table with Derrick following him to the church basement. The stairs down to the basement were unsteady in places, and some of the screws had worn loose over time from the handrail's wall anchors.

Derrick looked around casually. The basement social hall, though clean, was in need of repair. The kitchen refrigerator's door was cracked, as was the small oven.

Father Callahan observed Derrick's curious inspection.

"This kitchen is older than Mount Everest — a miracle it's still functional," he said. The basement hall had dozens of folding tables and chairs stacked neatly against yellowed, peeling walls.

"Someday this place will be back in tiptop shape," Callahan said hopefully.

"I could help you do that," Derrick piped up. "I'm real good with my hands, can fix most anything. My grandpa was a carpenter, taught me how to build most anything. And I'm a damn good mechanic."

Callahan wondered why this young man with so much talent lived on the streets.

As if reading his mind, Derrick said, "I've been fucked up since the war, can't hold down a job for too long."

"That was then and this is now," Callahan said. "I've been filling in as the church janitor. Might you be interested in doing my job?"

Derrick squeezed out his breath. "No problem. I'll do whatever you want, gladly."

"You can live here in this basement. There's a small room in that corner. It's been used by janitors off and on through the years. I'll ask Rosemary to keep this pantry and refrigerator up to snuff. In fact I'd like you to eat in the rectory with me, and when the church gets more money I'll pay you a respectable wage."

"Seriously?"

"Indeed. Take a look at this small bedroom. It has a shower, and your linens will be changed weekly. This bedroom door is secure."

Derrick sank heavily on the bed, teary-eyed. "You don't know shit about me," he said. "Hell, I could be a criminal on the FBI's most wanted list."

"I'll know what I need to know soon enough," the priest said, chuckling. "Unload your duffel bag, use the closet and dresser. I'll be back in a few minutes." He headed up the stairs, and on instinct turned around and saw Derrick taking clothes out of a garment bag, carefully hanging a rose-colored shirt, black tie, black pants, and shiny loafers in the closet.

Father Callahan sank on the stairs. Who was this man? Taking a chance with Derrick under any circumstance would be like playing with fire. He could pretend he hadn't seen Derrick's clothes, or just confront him.

He crept back to the bedroom where the closet door remained wide open. Startled, Derrick faced him. The priest said with a grim face, "I find it rather peculiar that a homeless man has such a fine set of garments."

Derrick shrugged. "You'll hate me, and throw me out if I tell you the truth."

"No matter. Please explain yourself." Father Callahan pulled up a straight chair and sat in front of the man. He ground his teeth, waiting. Derrick decided to risk coming clean. He sighed and dropped his shoulders. "I'm a gigolo. That's what these clothes are for."

Hearing this admission, Father Callahan's body released considerable tension.

"It began out of the blue on a Saturday afternoon when I was taking a walk on Fifth Avenue. That's when a middle-aged woman in a Thunderbird pulled up to me by the curb, and asked if I wanted a ride.

"Man, her blouse was wide open, and her dress hiked to her navel. We spent the afternoon fucking our brains out in her swanky Fifth Avenue penthouse. She paid me a ton of dough, gave me referrals, and that's how this shit started."

He took note that Derrick was strikingly good-looking — his sandy hair, large brown eyes, inviting lips, and six-foot-one frame oozed sensuality.

Derrick grew tense, expecting at any second for the priest to tell him to get the hell out, but he pressed on. "It got me food, and a place to stay and clean up. That's what these clothes are for. Truth is, I hate fucking those women. I do it to survive. If you don't want me here, I'll leave. Thanks for the breakfast . . . and your generosity."

"I want you to know that I'm the last person on God's earth to judge you, or anyone for that matter." He rested his hand kindly on Derrick's shoulder. Derrick knew he was taking a chance when he asked, "Have you been with women?" His voice cracked, as he searched for a level playing field.

Both men searched each other's eyes. Father Callahan spoke, "In my young days in Ireland, I had been many things and worked as a nightclub bouncer near University College in Dublin. Lots of pretty girls wanting us young men," he said easily.

Derrick's lips curled ever so slightly. This priest was not from the usual cut of cloth, that was for damn sure.

Father Callahan understood Derrick's need to probe, and he wondered if he were in the man's situation if he would have done worse.

"I want you to stay here, and I pray to God no harm shall come to your beautiful spirit."

"Beautiful spirit?" Derrick looked past him, embarrassed and saddened. "Beautiful — perhaps before death. I want to begin my work now, before you change your mind about hiring me," he said.

"Don't count on that," Callahan said with a smile as he pulled out brooms, pails, and other cleaning supplies from the work closet.

Derrick took a pail in hand, his eyes brightening. "Man, oh man, this arrangement is unbelievable." He filled a bucket with water.

Taking a risk with Derrick felt strangely normal after being cursed to damnation by a drunken priest. Derrick's remark that he might be trusting a criminal flashed briefly through his mind, but he dismissed it like the buzz of mosquitos.

He left the church basement and headed to the rectory, when a tall young woman wearing black, three-inch high heels called to him.

"Father, do you have any more large votive candles?"

Her voice was light and musical. Her auburn hair reached to the middle of her slender back. She moved closer to him, and her jasmine perfume draped over him like a sensual veil.

He inhaled deeply, taken aback; she could pass for his late wife with her deep blue eyes and full, inviting lips. Her bright face had no trace of makeup, and her snug sweater advertised a tantalizing femininity. He found himself alarmed by the excitement he began to feel in his lower extremities.

"Sorry, those candles won't arrive until the end of the week." He edged slowly away.

"My name is Bernice White."

"Father Callahan," he said.

"I want to talk to you about the greenhouse. My grandparents built and cared for it years ago."

"We can do that, but not now," he said. "I'm late for a meeting."

She pressed herself to his side and kissed him softly on both cheeks, in the French custom. "Till then," she purred, and turned to leave. He watched her glide gracefully to her yellow Ferrari, her skirt lifting as she slid into her car, revealing long, shapely legs. "God help me," he murmured, alarmed at his reaction.

* * *

Rosemary sat by the large bay widow with the sun warming her face, knitting a blue sweater for her five-year-old nephew. "I've just hired Derrick to be our church janitor. He'll live in the basement for the time being. He'll do a fine job," he said casually.

She stopped knitting.

"Have you no concern about Father Alex's reaction? It's like you've become the pastor."

He stiffened. "That crazy phantom is never around."

"Phantom? Not even close when it comes to you. He hates you worse than sin; I see the hate burning in those bloodshot eyes. Be careful of him," she warned.

"You have nothing to worry about."

But Rosemary did worry. She worried a lot.

Callahan went to his room, lying flat out on his bed and struggling to erase the memory of Bernice's kisses from his cheeks. They were in no hurry to be gone.

CHAPTER 7

He rested in front of the altar, enjoying the hypnotic flicker of the
votive candle before hearing this Friday afternoon's confessions
by school children, which gave him the greatest entertainment. He
especially enjoyed the confessions of nine-year-old Teddy, perhaps his
most outrageous penitent.

He heard Teddy bound down the aisle and into the confessional,
jumping up and down like a kangaroo on the kneeler.

"Bless me, Father," he began cheerfully. "I've done mortal sins."

"What might they be today?"

"I committed fornication and adultery."

Father Callahan quickly brought his hands to his mouth, forcing
himself not to roar with laughter. "And who are these women you've
sinned with?"

"It's a secret."

"What else?"

"Es . . . es . . . pionage?"

"And what kind of espionage might that be?"

"Very complicated," Teddy said, searching for the right words.

Father Callahan found it difficult to keep up a serious tone.
"Perhaps you have some simple venial sins to confess?"

"Nope, just mortal sins." Teddy pounded his chest contritely.

"How about lying, cheating and disobeying your parents?"

"Not important."

"For your penance, consider confessing these so-called
unimportant sins next time. And for God's sake, whatever stinks in
your lunchbox, get rid of it outside."

Father Callahan peeked out of the confessional to watch Teddy
skip down the aisle, dropping candy wrappers along the way. A
free, sinless child with a love for reciting outrageous sins from his
catechism book. He laughed until his sides hurt.

For the next fifteen minutes the church was quiet. A short time later he left for a game of poker with Derrick, which had become their early Friday evening ritual.

* * *

Derrick had a large bowl of salted, buttered popcorn sitting on the card table alongside a pair of root beer floats. "Today I will be the king of poker," Derrick announced, winking.

In the background a baseball game blared from his small TV.

"Who's ahead?" Father Callahan asked.

"The Yankees in the eighth, so far beating the Reds six to five."

Callahan didn't care for baseball, only soccer. He had played forward on his high school and college varsity teams — now a fading memory. He relished Friday evenings with Derrick, who had by now become, at six years younger, more like a kid brother. In no time the popcorn and root beer floats disappeared.

* * *

He returned to the church to hear confession, as he did from seven to eight every Friday evening. A young woman had entered the confessional, and through its thin, veiled curtain he watched her struggle to kneel. She was weeping heavily, her sobs punctuated with heavy wheezing that caused her to slide off the heavy wooden kneeler to the floor.

In alarm, Father Callahan threw back the heavy purple drape. "My god, child, you're in bad shape. Allow me, please, to take you to hospital."

"I'll be okay. Just don't leave me." She fumbled frantically through the contents of her purse. Coins, cosmetics and Kleenex tissues fell to the cracked floor and scattered. Her hands trembled like leaves in a windstorm. She grabbed her inhaler, squeezing it in her mouth as she gasped for air with desperate gulps. He lifted her gently to her feet as she regained control of her breathing a few moments later.

"Come with me to the sacristy. I have water there and a comfortable chair."

"Thank you," the woman said. She sank heavily in the armchair, taking deep slurps of water from a paper cup. She helped herself to a box of tissues, and wiped her puffy eyes.

He saw that she was a petite, shapely young woman, probably in her twenties. "I'm Father Callahan," he said softly. "Feeling a tad better?"

His sympathetic demeanor appeared to boost her confidence. "I'm Robin," she said timidly. "My Catholic girlfriend swears confessions are helpful even for those not Catholic."

"Many non-Catholics seek the consolation of confession," he said reassuringly. "What brought on this alarming asthmatic attack?"

Tears dripped down her pale, freckled cheeks. He bent forward in his chair anxious to hear her response, then drew back in shock when she rolled up her jeans. Her legs were covered in black and blue welts. She unraveled a thick, yellow scarf, exposing scabs and cuts that covered her neck. She then lifted the bottom of her thin blouse, where stripes of purple lesions covered her sunken stomach.

"My god, child. Who did this to you?"

Robin bent over, coughing as saliva dripped down her chin. She began gasping again, and hastily pushed the inhaler back into her mouth and sucked in more deep breaths.

Father Callahan jumped from his chair and went to her side. "Lassie, let's get you to hospital."

"I'll be all right," she said, slowly regaining control of her breathing.

"I want to help you before your injuries become infected. Who the devil did this to you?" His eyebrows pinched tight.

"Rubin Heckler, the bastard I live with," she said, heartened by his concern. "At first he was real nice, and talked me into moving in with him. After I did, my life went to hell."

"How so?"

"He began beating me!"

Father Callahan drew in a deep breath. "I noticed you've been rubbing your ribs?"

"I think Heckler broke them — hurts terrible."

He took a moment, then asked, "How does he hurt you?"

"He uses sticks and leather belts, ties me up. Gets a hard-on when I beg him to stop." She pulled the scarf to her face, sobbing.

Callahan held her hands gently as if she might shatter like a china doll.

"Lassie, I fear this horrid wretch will kill you — sooner rather than later. You've got to pack up and get out of his place as soon as you leave this church."

"I've tried. It took me a year to save enough money to get the hell gone. I hid all my money in my cosmetic case, planning to leave town tomorrow and take a bus to New Jersey and live with my Aunt Bessie."

"That must have taken hard work," he said.

She wiped her nose.

"Yeah. I'm a bartender at a cheapo strip club. It takes months to save a dime. That bastard went into my dresser drawer this morning and stole all my money."

No surprise there, Callahan thought. "Does he work?"

"He says he's an electrician, comes and goes all times of the day. God, how I despise him."

"Quite frankly, I don't understand why you've remained with the likes of this monster."

"'Cause he threatens to break my hands. I wouldn't be able to work. Now I'm penniless."

"Did you confront him?"

Her voice broke like glass.

"A real big mistake. He beat me senseless this morning and raped me. I'm hurting something awful," she said.

Father Callahan took her hands and gently brought them to her lap.

"Is there someone you can stay with as soon as you leave here?"

"My girlfriend."

"Please pack your clothes and get out of his apartment immediately," he said. "I wonder, have men always treated you so badly?"

She buried her face in her hands. "My stepfather used to beat and rape me after I turned eleven. I ran away from home at sixteen. My Aunt Bessie took me in."

"How about boyfriends?" he asked, hoping she wouldn't clam up.

"No one like Heckler. I gotta leave now. My shift at the bar starts in a couple hours."

With enormous effort and Father Callahan's help, she lifted herself out of the armchair. He wanted to draw her close to his heart and comfort her, as would a loving father.

"Promise me that you'll move in with your girlfriend before you go to work this evening, and see a doctor about your ribs and those other injuries. You don't want them to get worse."

She sniffled, no promise forthcoming.

"Lassie, I don't want to read about your demise in the New York Daily News."

"You're the only man who's given a damn if I lived or died," she whimpered.

He scribbled his phone number on a scrap of paper. "Call me day or night for anything."

She put his phone number in her purse next to her inhaler. "I will," she said thinly, with no conviction in her voice. She dreaded leaving the priest and the peaceful security of the old church, but she set off limping and turned painfully toward the bus stop.

Callahan watched her leave, fearing for her life and disheartened he could not shelter or protect her. He questioned whether God cared for her, then chastised himself for his lack of faith. In his gut he felt Heckler was a depraved freak and, given the opportunity, he would enjoy beating him to an inch of life, as he had done in another life on the streets of Belfast.

As Robin limped away, Father Callahan's advice repeated in her head, *Get away from Heckler fast. Stay with a friend. Your life is in danger. Do it now*. He had given her hope.

"I'll get back to the apartment, call my girlfriend, pack my clothes, and get the hell out," she thought. She pushed the inhaler to her lips, still shaking like a leaf.

Rubin Heckler watched her leave the church.

"Can't believe the bitch caught religion," he muttered to himself, snickering. He had followed her to the church and waited in his truck for her to leave. He drove back to his apartment, prepared to punish her and to hear her beg for mercy. The anticipation brought on an electrifying erection.

CHAPTER 8

Father Alex crept into Callahan's bedroom. The timing was perfect. Rosemary was shopping. The reprobate was in church saying private Mass. He left the bedroom door wide open, oblivious that Rosemary had returned from her shopping and was now in the pantry putting her groceries away.

She heard someone kicking and throwing things around in Father Callahan's room. Alarmed, she left the pantry and watched from the dining room, stunned. Alex was opening Callahan's small suitcase and tossing its contents onto the floor like so much dirt.

"I don't believe my eyes," she said to herself. She took off her shoes and tiptoed closer, being careful to stay hidden. She could hear him muttering crazily to himself.

Alex ripped open a sealed envelope containing Callahan's marriage certificate and his late wife's memorial papers. "Widowers be dammed," he shouted, "cursed to wear the holy cloth of the priesthood." He took Callahan's gold wedding rings to the window, inspecting them in the sunlight, then slipped them back into their pearl satin pouch and pushed them deep into his own cassock pocket.

Rosemary tore off her apron, ready to confront Alex, stopping only when she heard Father Callahan strolling through the breezeway singing "The Ferryman," his favorite Irish song. She retreated quickly to the kitchen, listening intently for what was to happen next.

Callahan froze at his door. His expression turned to stone. He stood dumbfounded as he saw Alex rifling through his personal papers like a feverish termite.

For some seconds Alex was oblivious to the presence of anyone else near him. Then Callahan kicked his bedroom door open with a thunderous crack.

"Get out of my room, you sick bastard!" he yelled as he clenched his fists.

Stupefied, Alex raced from the room, brushing Callahan aside. He fled upstairs and locked his bedroom door.

Callahan chased after him, taking the steps two at a time. He beat his fists on Alex's door. "How dare you invade my privacy!" he shouted.

He returned to his room. He was still breathing heavily as he began picking up his meager possessions. He stopped for a moment to rest against his dresser, when he discovered his precious wedding rings were missing. He ran back upstairs, kicking and pounding on Alex's door.

"Damn you, Alex, give back my rings."

Euphoric, Alex curled in his bathtub in a fetal position, rolling back and forth and laughing hysterically. He had found a way to torment the snake.

Rosemary, frazzled, had begun peeling potatoes for supper when Callahan approached her.

"Did you see Alex go through my possessions?" he asked, refusing to call him Father.

She nodded. "I was about to try stopping him when I heard you coming through the breezeway," she said, her face pinched tight.

"I'm sorry you had to witness this. What I need immediately is a locksmith. Know anyone?"

"Mike's Locksmith is very reasonable." She handed him a card from her purse. "I know it's not my business, but there are wonderful parishes who would appreciate you, and you wouldn't have to put up with the likes of . . ."

Woofy had scurried under the dining room table during the uproar. Now Callahan snuggled her safely in his arms.

"I know that," he said quietly, stroking the pup's floppy ears.

Thoughts of the penitents he cared for the most flashed into his mind. Robin, Casey, Derrick, Sheila, and young Teddy, who'd leave half his sticky Milky Way candy bars in the confessional as a token of affection. He determined in his heart not to abandon them.

On my wife's grave I swear to God that devil Alex will not destroy me, he thought. In less than thirty minutes the locksmith arrived to install a lock on his bedroom door.

Callahan, still shaken by the strength of his own fury and the intensity of his growing hatred for Alex, knelt before the altar praying, "Lord, I am desperate for help."

He buried his head in his hands. He knew now that Alex was resolved to punish him as part of some crazed, diabolical scheme. It seemed just a question of who would destroy the other first. He vowed he would not be destroyed.

* * *

Darkness lifted early Saturday morning with the sun shedding light and grace on New York City. Foghorns boomed from the Hudson River, and Father Callahan wondered if he would ever get used to them, let alone enjoy them the way so many New Yorkers did.

He dressed in preparation for today's visit to Monk Thron. For the trip, he wore casual pants, a loose shirt, and sandals without socks. He put Woofy in the back seat of the Chevy along with her toys, food and a doggy blanket, and started the leisurely drive to the Catskills, where the Zen monastery he sought was tucked into the mountains.

Autumn was busy doing nature's work of turning red maple trees into a breathtaking landscape filled with magical colors that lifted majestically through the mountain's landscape. He opened the car windows and inhaled the air's crisp freshness, welcome relief from New York City's dirt and din.

He stopped the car from time to time and got out to embrace the sweeping beauty of the mountain range. "This is where I should be living," he thought, but then rebuked himself for rebelling against God's will. He picked up a fallen leaf, still soft to his touch, and kissed it, rubbing it against his face. He put it carefully in the front seat of the car.

"I refuse to dry up and wither from lack of love," he vowed as he drove up a winding road flanked by balsam fir trees, whose ancient branches embraced him in a holy yet earthly welcome.

When he arrived at the monastery, a young monk in a white robe was greeting visitors of all ages. While he put Woofy on her leash, Father Callahan listened to the monk reciting a brief history of the monastery.

"This monastery was originally built by a Catholic priest," the monk explained, with no shortage of enthusiasm. Callahan listened with fascination near the tour group. The monk continued, "Norwegian craftsman used the area's bluestone and white oak to build these buildings, and through the years it became a Zen monastery." He led his group of devotees to the main building where they would spend the weekend in prayer, meditation, and spiritual exhortation.

The monastery's narrow cobblestone paths were filled with yellow Stella De Oro flowers woven among white daises nestled between bronze Buddha statues.

He relaxed on a wrought iron bench in front of a large copper bell that hung from an oval clay steeple by the monastery's front entrance, scolding himself for not making an appointment to visit with Monk Thron.

A moment later he heard a light tap on the bench's iron railing.

It was the monk himself.

"Have you been well?" Thron asked in an exceedingly soothing voice.

Father Callahan turned and met his gaze. The monk's face was radiant and seemingly ageless. He gently stroked Woofy's ears.

"Not healthy in my mind or heart," Callahan replied.

The monk smiled.

"I am Monk Thron, and pleased you have come to see me."

Thron chuckled at the astonishment that fell across Father Callahan's face.

"How do you know about my unannounced arrival?"

"I know many things," the monk replied. "That you are here is what matters." Father Callahan found himself at a loss for words.

"Come with me. Let us move through these holy paths and be touched by all that is sacred." The thin monk walked briskly ahead of Callahan, who found himself working hard to keep up with him. They wound their way up a hill for a mile until the monk pointed to an oak bench on which to rest.

Callahan sat beside the monk, struggling to collect his thoughts.

"I am . . ." he began, ashamed to acknowledge that he felt such a failure, that he had fallen so far from that period of grace he had spent as a Benedictine priest-monk in Ireland. He hesitated to expose his heart, even if that exposure might lead to understanding and healing.

The monk regarded Callahan reverently.

"Be not concerned. I am a human being, and my old feet have traveled long through life's years." He had no need to hurry, so he waited a long time until the young priest spoke.

It had taken time for the sickening tightness in Callahan's stomach to ease.

"Holiness seems like a distant star," he began haltingly. "I confess to despising my sadistic pastor, Father Alex. I live in despair, impotent to let go of people's suffering. I confess to wanting to kill, if given the chance, the sadistic boyfriend of a penitent who tortures her.

"I am the worst of impostors inside and out. I am in hiding from my contaminated past. I can't accept or deal with my present life. My sins are endless," he said, his voice cracking as he knelt before Monk Thron, who remained calm and serene.

"My dear son, you claim your sins are endless and beyond the mercy of Christ or Buddha?" he said in a playful, mocking tone. "Rise; do not kneel before me. Let us walk in peace a while longer." They moved silently up the winding path, greeted by birds' lively conversation, pausing from time to time to watch young deer jump between the bushes.

The monk offered Callahan water from his jug as they reclined on a slanted rock that was surprisingly comfortable.

"Tell me, what troubles you as a man?"

"As a man?" Embarrassed, Callahan cast his eyes past him.

"Yes . . . as a man. You have traveled long to converse with me. Now is the time to open your heart completely."

"I feel that you've been too long a monk to understand me."

"I understand many things," the monk said. He pulled a yellowed photo from a pocket in his robe and slid closer to the priest. "Look."

In the photo was a young pretty woman. "My wife."

"I was preparing to become a Zen Buddhist monk until I met sweet Lu and married her at eighteen. She was my heart, my soul. Two years later she died from a rare infection."

"I am so sorry," Callahan said. Monk Thron pulled out more photos. These are the monks I lived with."

"They look like children," Callahan observed.

"Some were." He opened another envelope, worn at the edges, and pointed to the larger photo he pulled from inside. "My parents, and my four sisters."

Callahan inspected them more closely. "They are so beautiful."

"Yes, there were." His eyes darkened. "All killed by Vietcong in Saigon. I had left many years before the war to abide in prayer and service at this sacred monastery."

"My God! Forgive me for judging you."

"There is no need, my son." He carefully put his hallowed photos back in his pocket.

"Tell me, what is wounding your spirit?" The monk asked.

Callahan inhaled deeply.

"My troubles are a frail shadow compared to what you have endured."

"Let there be no shadows or futile comparisons between us."

Callahan wiped his eyes with the end of his sleeve.

"I feel responsible for my pregnant wife's death. She was a terrible driver but late for a medical appointment, and she insisted on driving alone. I warned her not to take the back road with all of its squirrely cliffs in all directions."

Callahan rose from the rock, pacing back and forth.

"My wife was driving too fast around a steep bend, when the car swung out of control and dropped hundreds of feet down the cliff. She was killed on impact. It was my fault. I used to drive her everywhere."

"Ah . . . so you have been punishing yourself by becoming a priest and a monk, doing a life sentence of penance in a monastery and now living in a city parish and in a strange country."

"You believe I became a priest-monk to live a life of atonement for my wife's death?"

Monk Thron nodded.

"In your heart, my son, you know why. But what matters is what your motivation is today. The strength of your commitment to love and serve God today is what is important."

"I fear that whatever I do will never be enough," Callahan replied.

"In time your wounded heart will heal, according to your will. You have chosen a less traveled road, my son. Let us remember that life, at best, is fraught with suffering and mystery. Do not waste your precious life by withering in fruitless guilt and needless punishment."

"Holy man of God, I want to explain what happened to me."

Monk Thron folded his hands in a steeple. "I desire to be of service," he said bowing his shaven head toward Callahan.

"In the funeral home after my wife's accident, I tried to pull her body out of the casket. I was crazed from grief and guilt. The funeral director and others had to drag me away.

"Six months later I decided that by becoming a priest I could make amends for my wretched life and for my wife's death. It was then I became a diocesan priest.

"After just a year teaching in a Catholic high school, I was restless and unhappy. I needed to get out of Dublin. The city had become a place filled with memories of my wife. The Benedictine monastery accepted me and gave me the peace I desperately needed."

"And were you happy living in that monastery?"

"Yes, for three years I was very happy, until I was banished from Ireland by the monastery's new abbot, who hated me. He made sure to send me to a rundown New York City parish but also told the bishop of the New York Diocese that I was not to say public Mass, or preach, or to be in the company of women, and should be watched as if I were a venomous snake," Callahan said, his voice shaking.

"I do not think your abbot and I would enjoy each other's company," the monk said with a smile.

"Will my life ever get easier?"

"That depends on what you mean by easier," Monk Thron said.

"I still want the love, the tenderness I once had with my wife, and to become a father. Both now impossible."

"We are both brothers in suffering," Monk Thron added.

"But your suffering has been so much greater than mine," Callahan insisted.

"There is no such thing as greater or smaller. Making comparisons about our individual suffering increases suffering."

"But you are without fault. My life is contaminated."

Monk Thron's laughter lifted lightly through the pinewoods. "Be so grateful that you are young and alive. Best to suffer from being alive than from a life walking among the dead."

Callahan unexpectedly felt lighter. The monk's laugh, his wisdom and understanding, were beginning to soothe the raw wound he had kept locked for years inside his heart.

As they began a steady descent to the monastery, Callahan began a fervent, jumbled statement of thanks for the monk's help.

"There is no need," the monk replied cheerfully. "And healing is not a matter of rushing." He turned abruptly and nearly sprinted toward a group of visitors who had just arrived.

CHAPTER 9

Rosemary was delighted to see Father Callahan return. Deep down, she had begun to worry that he would not come back.

"Have a restful trip?" she asked.

"Getting away was what I needed. Have you ever visited that Zen monastery in the Catskills?"

"Never."

"Someday you must. It's a wonderland of beauty and peace."

Rosemary noticed a flash of wistfulness cross his face, and wondered if he would want to live up there, or return to Ireland.

As they spoke, the doorbell rang.

"I'll get it," he said.

Standing before him at the door was Bernice White. She was wearing a short, yellow sleeveless dress and sandals. She smiled.

Although Callahan was not pleased to see her, he managed a smile. "Come into the living room," he said, waving her in.

Bernice sank low in the old couch, crossing her long, slender legs, her dress lifting higher. He sat across from her and focused on her face, telling himself to grow up and be a man, be a priest. Sexy women are everywhere. *Don't get so caught up with this one*, he thought.

"I apologize for not being available the other day," he said.

"I know you were busy. I'm here because I want to do volunteer work for the church. The greenhouse was glorious when my grandparents built it. It's such a shame the way it's gone to rot." She wrinkled her eyebrows.

"I trust that will change," Callahan said.

"I used to be a bank manager at Goldmont Savings and Loan, until my grandparents died, and they left me a bundle. My working days are long over," she laughed, weaving her fingers gracefully through her silky, chestnut hair.

"I don't want to put you out, Father, but I'd like to see the inside of the greenhouse."

"There's really not much to see. I had it cleaned to the bone recently. It was in dreadful shape."

"That doesn't matter," she said.

They walked together to the back of the rectory. Father Callahan opened the greenhouse door tentatively and stepped aside, allowing her to enter, and watched as she ran a hand over the rotting shelves.

"My grandmother — Lord rest her precious soul — often took me here as a child," Bernice whispered as if they were in church. "I used to help my grandma put flowers in pretty vases for the church services." She turned to face Callahan squarely. "Tell me, when do you plan to have the greenhouse restored?"

"Not for a while. It's far too expensive."

Bernice took a checkbook from her leather clutch purse. "How much will it cost?" she asked as she poised a pen over an open check.

"Quite honestly, I haven't the slightest idea."

She put her checkbook back in her purse.

"If you're agreeable, I can get an estimate from a contractor the first thing tomorrow and see what's entailed, if that's all right with you?"

"No problem," he said, ignoring the fact that it was not within his official capacity to make this decision.

"Wonderful!" she gushed.

He walked Bernice to her bright yellow Jaguar, and opened the front car door. With no trace of shyness Bernice remarked, "I'm rather surprised a looker like you has embraced the celibate life of a priest."

Taken aback, he burst out laughing.

"The priesthood isn't just for the so-called plain and ugly," he said, his face turning a deep shade of red.

Her foot heavy on the pedal, Bernice raced off and flashed him a naughty wink.

Callahan chuckled again in spite of himself. Bernice was an irreverent handful. Her sensual presence lingered long after she had left, arousing him uncomfortably.

Monk Thron's exhortation, that it was better to be young and alive than to live among the dead, buzzed in his mind. Maybe being just a bit dead might not be all that bad, he thought.

* * *

Bernice drove leisurely to her Park Avenue apartment, nestled among the residences of the rich and famous. Thoughts of the greenhouse project quickened her heartbeat. She also thought about Father Callahan and wondered how much longer he would remain pure and undefiled.

* * *

Sheila fiddled with her purse handles as she waited opposite Father Callahan's confessional. Finally an elderly penitent shuffled out.

She pulled back the drape and knelt on the rock-hard kneeler.

"How have you been?" he asked, surprised she had returned, given their cantankerous exchange days past.

She smacked her gum loudly until he barked, "You are in the confessional. Please remove your gum." She pulled the wad from her mouth and stuffed it into a Kleenex tissue. She cleared her throat.

"It's about time Glenn Hudson leaves his wife and marries me like he's been promising."

Father Callahan half rose from his chair.

"My God, girl. How can you think for one solitary second that the attorney general of New York State, who has a wealthy wife and children, contemplates marrying his mistress? How will that happen, even in your delusional life?" He could feel heat rising in his throat. "All that creep wants from you is sex. It begins there and it ends there."

"No . . . no, you don't understand. It's so much more than that. Glenn loves me."

"Pay attention to me," he hissed, exasperated.

She fiddled in her purse, putting on perfumed lipstick and smearing it thickly on her lips, half listening.

"Your lunatic fantasies will be the ruin of you," he said, barely able to control his frustration.

"Glenn adores me, and tells me he's going to divorce his wife."

"Listen to me, for God's sake," he said. "Hudson is an unscrupulous liar. The sooner you get that into your head, the better."

"How can you say possibly say such a thing? He showers me with gifts, and with money. He's taken me to Lake George for weekends. He weeps when he leaves me."

"Holy Mother of God! Have you not listened to a word I've said?"

Sheila seemed to pay no heed to Callahan's warnings.

"I'll get pregnant, that's what I'll do," she continued. "Then he'll have to marry me. I'm tired of waiting. I'm tired of promises."

"Girl, stop this nonsense. What you're planning to do will be the death of you. You'll live to regret it . . . if you live at all."

"You're such a sweet, dear man," she said, leaving the confessional.

He flew out of the booth and confronted her.

"Don't you ever tell me I'm a sweet, dear man! I'm not some stupid passive listener just because I am a priest. I'm not here to hold your hand and feel sorry for you. It's nauseating."

"But you're supposed to take my side," she said angrily.

"Absolutely not. And don't think about bringing your sorry self back here unless you're serious about taking my advice," he barked as he pounded the confessional door.

Sheila froze, stunned by his outburst.

"If you want someone to feel sorry for you, you came to the wrong priest. I'm not some fool you can manipulate. Leave now."

She ran down the aisle, weeping and swearing never to return. He rushed to the sacristy, his heart pounding. He sank in the armchair, drawing his breath in ragged gulps. It took quite a while for him to regain control of himself.

Forget Sheila. She'll never return. But there was a part of him that wanted her to come back so he could find a way to penetrate her knuckle head so she could rid herself of that creep Hudson.

Give it up, he told himself. Maybe he should think about living at the Zen monastery. He wasn't cut out to be a passive confessor, and he worried that things were only going to get worse.

Callahan looked at his old Timex watch. It was four in the afternoon, a time when in Ireland's Benedictine monastery he would be chanting the Divine Office with other priests and brothers, their voices lifted peacefully to the heavens above. After prayer he would return to the barn to feed his horses and the other animals. He would savor their earthy smell as much as he did the holy scent of incense and candles.

Slowly he lifted himself from his chair, feeling as though he had been beaten by a rubber hose. "God save me," he said and moved through the breezeway to the rectory, anticipating a hot cup of tea and tasty crumpets.

* * *

Alex had been pacing back and forth in the dining room, waiting for Callahan to arrive. When he did, Alex half jumped in the air, swinging Callahan's pearl pouch like a pendulum and shrieking like the devil himself.

Callahan lunged toward him, "Give back my rings!"

Alex's face contorted in an ugly sneer as he twisted the pouch in his bony hands. "Not until you give me that dirty dog that's hiding between your legs," he said.

Callahan felt Woofy's quivering body press heavily against his leg. A surge of rage came over him, tightening his body so tensely he could hardly breathe. After his wife's death, he had come to find solace in the ritual of kissing both their wedding rings before falling sleep, but now these sacred objects were in the hands of this madman.

"What do you intend to do with my dog?"

"I know someone who'll take care of her," Alex said, his beady eyes glowing.

"When you put my wedding rings in my hand, I'll give her to you," he said, with no intention of doing so. Rosemary moved around the corner of the dining room, listening to their angry confrontation.

Alex tossed Callahan's satin pouch high and wide of Callahan, exposing Woofy when the younger priest lunged to catch it. Alex snatched Woofy by the scruff of her neck, shaking her mercilessly. She growled and twisted, and dug her teeth into his hand like a wild dingo, drawing blood. Stunned, Alex dropped Woofy on the floor.

Callahan grabbed the dog and secured the rings in his pocket.

"Give that dog to me!" Alex howled.

"Not on your wretched life."

Callahan went to his bedroom and locked the door, put his precious rings in his top dresser drawer, then consoled his whimpering little friend.

Alex stormed into the kitchen and snatched a bottle of scotch from the top kitchen shelf. "I'll get Bishop Graham to get rid of that retch of a priest," he muttered, wavering on the stool. For a fleeting moment Rosemary felt sorely tempted to kick the stool out from under him.

"It's time you treat Father Callahan with respect," she said angrily.

"Respect? Never."

"You went too far invading his personal property and stealing his wedding rings. God only knows what you'd do with dear little Woofy."

"As pastor I am entitled to do what I please."

"I don't think so. Father Callahan could have tossed you down the stairs and stomped on you."

"I'll rid myself of all of you," Alex mumbled, slurping down some Scotch to dull a mind and heart that had once been sharp and kind.

Callahan had opened his door a crack and heard Rosemary say, "Be grateful he doesn't throw you down the stairs and stomp on you."

Callahan smiled.

CHAPTER 10

It had taken hours to get to sleep as he tossed and turned, thinking about wanting to beat the living daylights out of Alex, and about Sheila's stupidity. But eventually a recurring nightmare took hold of him. He found himself clawing his way down a razor-sharp cliff to reach his wife's mangled body, fighting to pour his life into her.

He woke drenched in sweat, and even more depressed. He got out of bed and filled his tub with hot water and soaked until he thought he would melt. Finally feeling better, he sank back into bed and slept.

* * *

Early the next morning Callahan watched workmen haul long sheets of redwood shelving into the greenhouse where Bernice was speaking to the contractor, thrilled with the start of the restoration. She wrote out a check for two thousand dollars and pressed it into the hands of the smiling contractor.

Then Casey opened the backyard gate and approached Father Callahan. His face was drawn and gray. "Gotta sec?"

"Certainly," Father Callahan replied.

Callahan welcomed the chance to leave Bernice. She had a habit of greeting those of choice with a too-friendly kiss from cheek to cheek, and that included him. He recently found himself backing off rather quickly with each new approach. It was an effort just to be around her. What's more, she had picked up the hint, and responded with a pout.

"Let's go to the sacristy—more private there," he told the detective. Casey followed on his heels, and once inside slumped in the armchair.

"You look like you've been sleeping in the morgue," Father Callahan said, a note of concern in his voice.

"Real close," he grunted. "Karen Ford — the daughter of my friend Tom Ford, who's police chief in New Rochelle — was murdered, raped and tortured in her Bronx apartment around two this morning."

"My God," Callahan gasped, placing his hand over his heart.

"I've known the Ford family for years. I was Karen's godfather. Two weeks ago her father paid big bucks for a high-end security system. Shit, the bastard broke into her apartment like it was soft putty. Fucking unbelievable!"

"I can't imagine what the family must be going through," Callahan said, biting the inside of his lip.

"No one can — that's for damn sure. Ford was supposed to take Karen to JFK Airport this morning to leave for a birthday trip to Paris. When she didn't show up or answer her phone, Ford drove to her apartment and found her . . ." Casey swore under his breath, his emotions raw.

"At five o'clock this morning Chief Duffy was banging at my door. When we got to Karen's apartment, police were swarming her place like locusts. Chief Ford was so freaked out, it took three officers to wrestle him down and grab his gun away from him. After that, they put him in Duffy's car. An officer was glued to his side."

Casey helped himself to a glass of water from a pitcher near his chair.

"Man, I had to force myself to go into Karen's apartment. Her piano had dozens of family pictures on it. There was one of me at her recent twenty-first birthday party."

"I'm so sorry," Callahan whispered.

Casey talked faster, his voice breaking in places.

"Damn, when I dragged myself into her little bedroom, there were three other officers in there, tighter than knots, poring over the death scene." Casey wiped his dripping forehead, his face flushed red.

"Take your time," Callahan said. "There's no need to rush."

Casey rose from his chair and leaned against the wall.

"Everyone was really wound up. Jackson, a forensics officer, shoved his fist practically into my face and warned me not to touch a fucking thing till he was gone. Remember, I'm just a friend of the family, a retired guy with no professional reason to be there, right? I plastered myself against the bedroom wall, trying to become invisible."

Impossible, Father Callahan thought. Casey was a bull of a man and built like a boulder.

"Karen's naked body was laid out on her bed. Her neck had been twisted and broken." Casey wiped his eyes. "Her arms were squeezed rigid to her sides; all of her fingernails were broken, and the bed sheets were drenched in blood. She must have fought like a tiger."

Casey dropped back into the chair, struggling to control himself.

"I tore out to the backyard and retched my guts out. I'm still queasy."

He downed another glass of water. "You gotta know . . . Karen was like a daughter to me. I watched her grow up into a beautiful young woman."

"How about going outside to get some fresh air. It might help."

"Padre, it won't do a damn thing for me.

"When the crime scene cops left, I put on latex gloves and searched Karen's room and dresser like a bloodhound. I was frantic to get it done before the FBI pounced and stripped Karen's place down to the nails."

Callahan refilled Casey's glass.

"I wish I could be of more help," he said.

"Padre, just you listenin' helps me deal with this shit. I don't have a cat, a dog or a hamster to pour my guts out to," he said with a thin smile.

"I'm glad," Callahan said, in spite of how helpless he felt inside. At least he was more useful than a hamster.

"When I opened Karen's jewelry case I wasn't sure what to look for. Ford was still sitting like a block of stone in Duffy's car, having watched his daughter's body being taken to the morgue for an autopsy.

"Man, the smell of blood and death hung so heavy in that small bedroom . . . like a suffocating plague. I sure as hell didn't want Ford going back in there. That's why I took Karen's jewelry case to him in the car. He could barely focus. I was about to leave when he mumbled, "I gave Karen a designer diamond ring for her birthday. It's missing."

"Maybe the assassin takes stuff from his victims . . . either to sell it or as some sort of demented trophy," Father Callahan said.

"Yeah," Casey said, "that's something I'm looking into."

"How is Chief Ford doing?" Callahan asked.

"Duffy drove Ford to the ER. He had passed out. Now he's on the mend from what they're calling a minor heart attack."

"Well, the recovery is at least a bit of good news," Father Callahan said.

Casey drained his third glass of water.

"It's a good thing I don't drink. I'd be in the tank by now. My father was a raging alcoholic—used to beat up my mother and me. I was sixteen when he went after my mom and I took a crowbar and near killed the son of a bitch. I've never taken a drink in my life."

Callahan nodded. "I used to drink like a fish as a young kid, until I got tired of being dragged to the hospital, deathly sick. Didn't take me long to give up the bottle. That's a blessing for both of us."

"Glad we have something in common . . . more than just religion," Casey said.

"I suppose Chief Duffy is giving you more help in your investigation now?"

"Don't I wish," Casey grumbled. "Not even a lowly crumb's slithered my way. He still worries about other cops getting wind of my investigation."

"You said he's worried about corrupt cops, but could he be worried that one of them is the killer?" Callahan wondered out loud.

"Don't think it hasn't crossed my mind," Casey said weakly, "but I can't find any evidence of that. And when a police chief worries about corrupt cops, it's more like issues of skimming cash or dope before it gets bagged for evidence. Not murder.

"I have started to look at cons and creeps who have a history of defeating security systems, guys who were arrested by cops in these jurisdictions who might have decided to take it out on the chief of each department that arrested them.

"But that's a wide search, and my progress is so damn slow, if you can even call it progress. If I could sit in a precinct for eight hours every day and run computer searches I would get farther. Instead, I have to tell the chief what I'm thinking, ask for the files that are sometimes filed away someplace pretty deep, and then wait for him to slip them to me.

"I have never felt so incompetent in my damn life. Girls are dying while I'm chasing my tail."

"So, no new leads from this latest crime scene?"

"Nothing. Same ol' shit. All we know for certain is that we're dealing with a serial killer who has a serious vendetta against high-level police officers and takes it out by murdering their daughters.

"He rapes, then strangles his victims. It's all particularly vicious. None of them so far have been over twenty-one — all petite young women, living alone, no pets. He breaks through their security systems like he designed the damned things, then murders his victims. Always around 2 a.m. . . . uses condoms, latex gloves . . . even shoe covers. He doesn't even leave tire marks outside."

Casey leaned back in his armchair and closed his eyes while the church bells echoed through the neighborhood.

Father Callahan's thoughts drifted back to the streets of Belfast. He was eighteen and running back home near midnight. He was taking a shortcut through an alley when he heard a girl scream for help.

He ran toward her cries and saw a British soldier raping her and punching her in the face. Callahan howled and ran at him, full throttle.

The soldier drew a handgun and fired a shot that grazed Callahan's ear.

In the heat of the moment he struggled for the gun and it fired again, hitting the soldier point-blank. He rolled the soldier's body off the girl and saw that she was no more than twelve. Knowing other soldiers would be coming, he swept her up and raced into the darkness. She eventually was able to mumble an address and he took her home. Out of gratitude, the IRA had welcomed him, and protected him from the British.

He snapped back to the present when Casey pounded the sacristy table.

"On my life, I swear to God, I'm gonna crucify this killer's ass."

Callahan realized that his own fists were clenched and his knuckles white. An edge of steel in his voice, he hissed, "I can help you do that."

CHAPTER 11

Alex had cloistered himself in his bedroom, reeking of booze. As a
rule, he forbade Rosemary from entering his room, even to clean.
She left his meals on a tray by his bedroom door. With the exception
of visiting the pantry to retrieve the scotch and wine that he ordered
weekly, he had become a living ghost. No one missed him.

During the past week, precisely at 9 a.m. each day, Bernice
had arrived at the rectory excited to supervise the restoration of the
greenhouse. Callahan greeted her briefly, admiring the steady progress
of workers putting their finishing touches on the greenhouse's new
redwood shelving.

Lily's Plant Service arrived, delivering potting soil and dozens of
pots filled with budding roses, daises, lilies, and ferns.

Bernice beamed, "The greenhouse will be completed this week."

"You've done a fine job," he said.

"Oh, but I want to do so much more. We could renovate the
rectory and the church. It's so old and shabby."

He frowned.

"I don't think anything's been done since the church was built,
but the expense involved would be enormous."

Bernice flung her arms in the air, laughing. "Expense of any kind
is no problem."

A sudden thought of Alex's likely reaction entered his mind. He
brushed it aside.

"Let's talk about it tomorrow," he said.

"Wonderful. I can hardly wait," she said, and hurried to the
greenhouse, where Lily's Plant Service was arranging rows of bright
yellow tulips.

* * *

As he strolled to the church basement, he wondered why Bernice was so generous. The rectory and church definitely needed a facelift. Being around her, though, would bring its own challenges. She would be spending hours in the rectory and church, and even the church basement. He would have no choice but to be around her. The thought was troubling.

He worried for Robin's safety, and was still fuming over Sheila's idiotic fantasies of getting pregnant. And Casey had phoned, still frantic to find the serial killer but with no breakthrough in sight.

A deadening sense of futility took hold of him. The idea that a confessor could or should listen passively was making less and less sense to him, and this notion tormented him every time he entered the curtained confessional.

His thoughts drifted to the peaceful serenity of the Zen monastery and Monk Thron.

CHAPTER 12

Light rain freshened New York City in the early morning while Callahan inspected the saintly statue of Saint Francis of Assisi, sheltered near the church's front doors. The rain peeled city grime off the concrete buildings, lazily draining into gutters and lifting his mood as he filled his lungs with autumn's crisp freshness.

For a spell he played Woofy's favorite game of hide-and-seek. She tore around the greenhouse, then jumped into his arms to announce that the game was over and it was time for a doggy treat.

After putting her in his room he entered the confessional and left the door of his booth slightly ajar, peering at folks who simply dropped in to light a candle, no doubt praying for a miracle. Some people dropped a scant few coins into the collection box and vanished back to their city lives.

He saw Robin walking down the aisle from the back of the church, coughing and sniffling. She pulled back the confessional drape and gripped its outer ledge, kneeling painfully down. "It's Robin," she whispered hoarsely.

"I thought by now you'd be long gone from the city and away from that cockroach Heckler!"

She wrung her hands nervously.

"He followed me here the last time I came, and he beat me when I got back to the apartment. He swore he'd kill me if I came back to see you."

Father Callahan easily saw her swollen, black-and-blue face through the veil. Seeing her this way sickened him.

"My God, child, if you don't leave that monster, he'll kill you sooner than later. Believe me, lassie, I'm serious about your dangerous situation."

"I can't think about leaving now. I have no money." She pulled back the confessional drape and looked around to see if Heckler had followed her into the church. She was a nervous wreck.

"Do you think he's hiding close by?"

"Could be."

"I'm going to check it out," Callahan said, "What kind of a car does he drive?"

"A red Ford truck."

He looked up and down the aisles, then hurried down the church steps, searching in every direction. The creep was nowhere to be seen. Still, he could be hiding in a nearby alley or in the corner of a storefront.

Back at the confessional he said, "Wait here a moment. I'll be right back." He ran to his room and stuffed two months' worth of his meager wages into an envelope. "Please take this," he said.

She slipped the money into her purse, trembling.

"I'll pay you back," she said.

"Please don't think about doing that."

"I have to pack my clothes. I don't have much."

"I fear if you return to that apartment alone, Heckler might be there, itching to harm you, for God's sake. Do you have any male friends who can accompany you back there?"

"All the guys I know are working. My girlfriend Rachel lives across the bridge in Jersey. She told me I could stay with her."

"That's a good thing. I'll drive you to the apartment. You definitely need protection. After you pack your things, I'll take you to your girlfriend's house."

She lifted her pale, freckled face.

"You mean to say you'd do that for me?"

"Absolutely. I want you to be among the living and not among the dead," he said with a small smile.

"What if Heckler's there?" she asked, beginning to shake.

"You have nothing to fear. I'll handle what needs handling."

"But you're just a priest. Heckler's a dangerous maniac. He's very, very strong."

"Lassie, don't fret."

They arrived in the Bronx at a low-end neighborhood where small houses were stuck between tottering gray apartments. Young children played in the streets as their mothers watched from their porches and windows.

"That's his place," Robin said, pointing to Apartment 12-B, situated on the first floor of an old building at the end of the block. Instinctively, they looked right and left for Heckler's red Ford truck — nowhere to be seen.

"We gotta hurry," she said, panicked. "Rubin could come back at any time."

They entered his apartment, which was close to bare. A worn leather couch sat low in the living room before a small TV set. A queen-size bed with a thin, yellow cover took up most of the bedroom. He looked in the closet and drew back, startled. Heckler had few clothes, which struck him as odd, as though Heckler had secrets and didn't really live here.

Robin frantically threw her clothes into a small suitcase, not bothering to fold them. Minutes later Callahan smelled the stink of a cigar and spun around.

Heckler glared at them through the bedroom doorway.

"Who the hell are you?" he shouted.

Robin grabbed Father Callahan's jacket, terrified.

"He's my friend. He's a priest. He's taking me away so you can't torture me no more."

In seconds, both men had sized each other up — each about six-one and well built. Heckler sneered at the priest and lurched toward Robin. Callahan grabbed his arm, slamming him against the wall.

"Robin, get out of here — get in my car," Callahan yelled.

Robin raced out of the apartment with her suitcase. Heckler swung his fist at Callahan's gut, but slipped on the throw rug and fell to the floor.

"Coward," Callahan roared, "beating a helpless woman! He kicked Heckler fiercely in the back. Heckler lay still for a moment, stunned at the priest's ferocity.

"You can end this right now, Heckler, or you'll have hell to pay."

It didn't matter. Heckler sprang up and punched Callahan hard in the jaw, knocking him down. Heckler lifted his foot to crush him in the groin but Callahan was faster. He grabbed Heckler's leg and threw him against the dresser. When Heckler fell to the floor, Callahan pounced and pounded his jaw.

Robin couldn't stand the tension a second longer, fearing for the priest's life. When she opened the apartment door, Heckler was flat on his back with Callahan's knees pressed on his stomach. The priest pounded Heckler until the pervert was completely still.

Father Callahan got up, winded.

"I hate you!" Robin screamed. She took off her shoe and started smashing it on Heckler's nose. Blood gushed down to his mouth.

"Did that feel good, lassie?" Callahan asked.

"Sooo good. Where did you learn to fight like that?"

"In Belfast."

"Belfast, Maine?" she asked.

He laughed, "Not even close. Let's get out of here. It won't be pretty when that slug gets up." They hurried to the car as Robin screeched with laughter.

* * *

He drove Robin across the bridge to New Jersey, parked his car and carried her small suitcase to her friend's house. The neighborhood was quiet. Large maple trees shed red and yellow autumn leaves on thick, green lawns, a welcome change of scenery from New York's concrete vistas.

"Any plans for your future?" Callahan asked, rubbing his throbbing jaw.

"Tomorrow I'll take a bus to Somerville, New Jersey. That's where my Aunt Bessie lives. She manages the Beacon Country Club restaurant; that's where I'll be working."

"No more bartending?"

"That's over . . . forever. I'm going to take evening college courses. I want to be a nurse," she said, and her face lit up at the prospect.

"Good for you."

"You saved my life," she said.

"Truth be told, you may have done me a favor. I rather enjoyed beating the crab out of that creep," he said with a chuckle.

She pressed his money back in his hands. "I won't be needing this." She rose on her tiptoes, kissing him lightly on his cheek.

As he drove back to the rectory, he prayed that Robin would find a worthy man who would love and marry her. She deserved nothing less. For the first time since he had arrived in New York City, he felt he had accomplished something worthwhile.

Upon reflection, he realized that in Belfast it would have been easy to punish Heckler further, to within an inch of his miserable life, or even to kill him. His hands on the wheel began to shake when he fully realized just how easy that would have been today — even though he was now a priest, a man of God. Still, the more he thought about their hand-to-hand combat, the better he felt.

CHAPTER 13

Rosemary had taken an affectionate liking to Bernice. Often they chatted in the dining room over tea and pastries. This didn't sit well with Callahan. He wanted Bernice gone after she finished her work in the greenhouse. Today when he entered the rectory, Rosemary called to him, "How about joining us?"

He sat stiffly next to Bernice and watched the steam from his teacup float lazily in the air. "More flower seedlings are arriving tomorrow," she announced cheerfully. "Don't you think the greenhouse volunteers are doing a excellent job?"

"They are," he said, getting up from the table, anxious to get away from her.

"Please come with me. I want to show you how well the flowers are thriving." Reluctantly he walked behind her, noticing the swinging of her hips. Her yellow sundress lifted with every step she took. He inhaled the delicious aroma of her perfume, a new and equally tantalizing scent each day.

Bernice looked forward to sitting next to him at the dining table. She enjoyed the huskiness of his voice, the sensual movement of his lips, and his boyish laughter. She wondered if he took notice of her as a desirable woman, and if he would be as ravishing a lover as she sensed. Her body had grown wet with desire from her fantasies, calming to a reasonable degree only as they entered the greenhouse.

"Take a look at these gorgeous pink orchids. They're used only for special occasions," she gushed.

"You're doing an outstanding job," he said, admiring the long rows of lilies, roses, pansies, and vegetables thriving from care. The new redwood shelves, now sparkling clean, were a tribute to Bernice's diligent management.

Seemingly out of the blue she tripped. Callahan caught her before she fell to the ground. Her breasts rubbed softly against his hands, exciting him. These damn temptations will never end, he thought, upset.

"This greenhouse ground needs to be leveled—far too uneven," she complained. Actually, she couldn't have cared less. It was his strength and the excitement she felt from his body that gave her hope.

The greenhouse grounds seemed perfectly level to him. He hated to think Bernice might be playing with him. The touch of her breasts against his hands awakened far too many memories.

* * *

Father Alex had watched Bernice and Father Callahan conversing from his bedroom window. He opened his diary, thrilled to make another entry. In due time he would place his precious diary in the hands of Bishop George Graham, who was in charge of internal affairs for the New York archdiocese.

"I witnessed Father Callahan kiss and move his hands over Bernice's breasts. I saw him pull down her panties in plain daylight," he wrote. "They were alone in the greenhouse for hours. Dated Wednesday, October 20, 1979, at 1:00 a.m."

He counted the days until Father Callahan would be excommunicated, disgraced, and banished to the pits of Ireland.

* * *

Rosemary called to Father Callahan from the doorway of the greenhouse.

"You have a phone call," she said, then fled quickly back to the rectory. He hurried to take the call, still sweating profusely from his awkward encounter with Bernice.

The gentle voice of Monk Thron greeted him. "At the hour of noon I shall visit you," he said pleasantly.

"Wonderful" Callahan said. The timing was perfect, and he waved good-bye to Bernice.

When the church bells tolled at noon, Monk Thron arrived in an old white Buick driven by a head-shaven young monk. When the car came to a stop he bounded out of like a child.

"I'm happy you've come," Callahan said. "Your driver could have stayed for lunch."

"There is no need," Thron replied, "Monk Thaddeus has many errands to care for. Rarely do we come to the city.

"My son, it appears there is still much troubling you."

They sat quietly on the rectory steps, until Callahan felt ready to confess his sins.

"I confess to losing control of myself. I beat up a man who abused, raped and beat his girlfriend. But when I did this, I didn't feel sorry. I felt strong and alive."

Monk Thron listened peacefully, his hands folded on his lap, and Callahan continued to pour out his sickness like a festering boil.

"When that sick fleabag Alex stole my wedding rings I also wanted to beat the crap out him, and only God knows what else I might do." He paused to catch his breath.

"And Bernice, that woman who just left, I want her in my bed with a level of lust that feels insane," he spurted, digging his fingers in his scalp.

"A lot of wants, young man," Monk Thron said with a small grin. He rose and swept his hands lightly over Callahan's head and heart in a sacred blessing.

"Your life is not evil. Every day is your destiny," he said.

"Destiny?"

"Yes . . . destiny."

"I don't understand."

"Understanding is a lifetime journey. Begin by forgiving yourself for not forgiving yourself and move forward moment to moment, in joy and peace."

The monk's driver had arrived.

"I shall return in time," Thron said, and he nearly skipped off to the car, leaving Callahan to deal with his own problems whether he wanted to or not.

After the holy monk had left, the burning pain from Heckler's punch to his jaw disappeared. Had the little monk cured it? How would he even known his jaw was killing him?

Upon reflection he realized he had been in the company of a holy man whose extraordinary powers seemed to come to him as naturally as breathing. The monk had quietly given him a blessing, a gesture of kindness and support.

He reflected on the monk's exhortation that "the journey of understanding takes a lifetime." The thought of a lifetime was frustrating; he had hoped for instant answers and instant solutions. But the monk's counsel to forgive himself for not forgiving himself was something he could sink his teeth into right now.

He returned to the church and opened the Bible, praying for patience and forgiveness. Was a life of faith possible only for the pure of heart? What about for him, a hard-core sinner who did indeed seem to be at home among sinners?

* * *

Alex called to Rosemary from the top of the stairs, dressed in smelly pajamas and tattered bathrobe.

"Who was that peculiar man dressed in gray robes talking to the reprobate?"

"A holy Buddhist monk," she answered sharply, upset that he referred to Father Callahan as a reprobate.

He opened his diary, writing excitedly. A heretical monk with destructive doctrines spent the afternoon talking with Father Callahan, who is clearly of like mind, fouling the holiness of my parish with his heretical presence and doctrine.

CHAPTER 14

A tall, slender man paused thoughtfully in front of Saint Francis of Assisi Church at 8:45 a.m. as parishioners, mostly old, entered the church for Sunday Mass. He leaned casually against the baptismal font nestled in back of the church, admiring the new walnut pews and white sanctuary carpets, surprising for a church too long teetering on bankruptcy.

He slid into a pew next to an elderly woman who was thumbing her pearl rosary beads and whispered, "I haven't been here for years. It looks likes the church has been renovated?"

"Indeed it has," she said brightly, studying the good-looking man with curly red hair in his long, gray trench coat. "Anonymous donations have been pouring in. Even that dump of a greenhouse has been restored."

"Really?"

"Yes," she whispered. "No one is supposed to know who the generous donor is."

"Might you?" he asked pleasantly.

"No harm, I suppose, in telling," she said as she buried her prayer beads deeper in her lap. "It happens to be the very wealthy Bernice White. She's also in charge of the greenhouse's flowers. The plants are even providing some food for the poor. She does a whole lot around here," she said, appreciating his keen interest.

"That's a good thing," he said, admiring the long-stemmed yellow roses in elegant crystal vases in front of the altar. "When does Mass begin?" looking at his watch.

"Father Alex, the pastor, is always late," she grumbled. "Supposed to begin at nine."

He took note that the altar did not face the people, as directed by the Vatican and the archdiocese. Finally, at 9:30, Father Alex staggered into the sanctuary. He began saying Mass in Latin, instead of in English, and did not give a sermon.

"Are there other priests in residence?" he asked.

"Just Father Callahan. He only hears confessions."

"Why is that?"

"Just some gossip . . . if you really want to know?"

"That suits me fine," he said, a twinkle in his eye.

"People think the old pastor is just plain jealous of him. He's a looker, and easy to like," she said, her eyebrows lifted.

"Not to be presumptuous, but I take it you don't like Father Alex?"

"Not much to like. The former pastor, Father Paul, was a true pastor. Time gone this church was filled to the gills," she said unhappily.

He watched, sickened, as Father Alex left the sanctuary, swaying from side to side. He counted twenty-four people in attendance, no families, no children; most were women past sixty. He reviewed the one-page Sunday bulletin that listed the times of confessions and the cost of lighting candles. There were no convert classes, no novenas, no youth groups or altar society. Zero activity was the depressing order of the day for this parish.

He left the church, curious, and went to the greenhouse. Opening the door and peering in, he was surprised to see a beautiful young woman putting flowers into straw baskets with yellow bows and round blue nametags.

"Sir, can I help you?" she asked with a generous smile.

"I am just looking," he answered politely. "A rather nice job you're doing here."

She reached out to shake his hand.

"I'm Bernice White."

"George," he replied simply.

"I haven't seen such a glorious redhead in years," she kidded cheerfully, enjoying his full-throated laughter.

"Glorious is fitting on my mother's side of the family, all from Scotland."

The fact she was a hard worker and a very generous benefactor was a hopeful plus for this church, he thought.

"I must be on my way," he said lightly.

"Please come back. I can use more volunteers, especially for delivering flowers and food to the homebound and homeless."

As he walked out through the backyard gate, a young man was leaving the church basement with a small, rambunctious dog pulling vigorously at its leach.

"Cute pooch you have there," he said.

"She's not mine," Derrick said. "Adopted by Father Callahan. Woofy's her name. I take her for walks from time to time."

Woofy pranced up to the stranger, sat on her small haunches, and presented him with a tiny paw.

He bent to shake it and she rewarded him quickly with a dainty lick on his nose. He chuckled, scratching her back. "Do you happen to work here?"

"Yep. I'm the church janitor, thanks to Father Callahan. He saved me from a really wretched life on the streets."

"I'm happy for you," the visitor said, and then watched them dash down the block.

Before getting into his Chrysler he glanced back at the front of the church where Father Callahan was greeting the parishioners as they left, noticing he often glanced over his shoulder toward the rectory as if worried he would be noticed.

Bishop George Graham tossed his trench coat along with the anonymous letters of complaint into the back seat, no longer smiling.

* * *

Callahan enjoyed washing his clothes on late Sunday afternoons in the church basement. Everyone had left for the day, and this was his special time to be himself and to let loose. Thanks to Bernice's boundless generosity the laundry room had a new washer and dryer, and a big white porcelain sink. He wore loose sweatpants and no shirt as he moved his damp clothes to the dryer.

Casey had been looking for him in the empty church and in the greenhouse. No one answered the rectory bell. He went to the basement and heard Callahan singing at the top of his lungs the Irish hit song "Spirits in the Sky," dancing from one end of the basement hall to the next, his feet flipping high in the air, lost in the thrill of dance.

Casey edged back up to the top of the stairs unseen, loathe to intrude on the priest's fun. When the laundry bell rang, Callahan stopped and took his clothes from the dryer with his naked back exposed to Casey.

The detective drew back, staring at a stunning tattoo of a Celtic dragon that extended from below Callahan's neck to his backside, edged in bright green and yellow. Taken aback, Casey returned home wondering who Father Callahan really was. It was the way he carried himself, the way he avoided Bernice, the way he was so much at ease with Derrick, and the manner in which he had said, "I can help you catch that killer." It was more than a little confusing.

Part of Callahan seemed like many young men Casey had dealt with over his career, delinquents, gang bangers and street fighters. He knew the type like he knew the mole on his cheek. Hell, he grew up on the streets of Queens, and in some ways had been one of them. But he couldn't get the Celtic tattoo out of his mind. Maybe Callahan had gotten it as a teenager. But it was an extraordinary piece of work and must have cost much more than a typical teenage thug could afford.

In his college days Casey had studied some art, and this tattoo fascinated him. Unable to control his curiosity, he hurried to his phone and placed a long-distance call to his cousin, a police captain in Belfast.

"Paul, you owe me a favor."

CHAPTER 15

He rang the doorbell at 3 p.m., briefcase in hand, anticipating an ugly visit. Rosemary's mouth dropped when she recognized Bishop George Graham from the diocesan newspapers.

"I trust I am not intruding," the bishop said.

"Not at all, Your Eminence. I am Rosemary, the rectory's housekeeper. May I take your coat?"

"Thank you."

"Shall I tell Father Alex that you are here? I doubt he is expecting you."

"Do tell him, and please show me to the office."

He entered the stuffy, airless room and proceeded to the desk. He bent over, blowing dust off piles of unopened letters that lay yellowing in wire baskets. He flipped through unpaid bills and letters from parishioners. The desk suffocated from neglect, as did the parish, he surmised. He was amazed the parish still limped along despite Bernice White's generous donations.

He opened his briefcase and placed his files neatly on top of the desk, waiting for Father Alex to appear. Rosemary beat on Alex's door like a set of drums. Alex was listening to his television blasting "Days of Our Lives," his favorite soap opera. Bishop Graham stepped out of the office, listening.

"Bishop Graham is waiting to see you in the office," Rosemary shouted.

It took a while before Father Alex opened his bedroom door a notch. "Who?"

"Bishop Graham," she repeated louder.

"I'll be down in a few minutes."

"Hurry," she said, shaking her head.

Bishop Graham paced back and forth in the office, his mood souring, until Father Alex entered the office, excited.

"I'm pleased you've come," he said, placing his journals eagerly on the desk.

Graham nodded, his eyes fastened on Alex's dirty bedroom slippers and smelly cassock. He drew in a harsh breath. He reviewed the letters and journal.

"You are accusing Father Callahan of taking over your parish responsibilities, and keeping a mutt in his room. Apparently, he hired a street derelict as the church janitor, housing him in the church basement, et cetera, et cetera, et cetera," he said, tapping his fingers irritably on the desk.

"Oh, but there is so much more," Alex said, thrusting another wine-stained journal in front of him, tightening his arms against his chest. Bishop Graham thumbed impatiently through the pages. "Father John has intimate relationships with Bernice White outside and inside the greenhouse. He seeks counsel from a heretical monk who lives in the Catskills."

Graham was growing more disgusted. He was sorely tempted to throw Alex's journals to the floor and stomp them to smithereens.

"You have an eternity of grievances," he said in a mocking tone.

Father Alex pressed on, heedless of Graham's indignation.

"Oh, I forgot to mention that he steals money from the church."

"I've heard enough," Graham said, running his fingers through his hair.

* * *

When Father Callahan arrived in the rectory from hearing confessions, Rosemary hurried to him, twisting her apron strings nervously. "You better prepare yourself for a load of trouble. Bishop Graham's been in the office with Alex for the past hour."

"Any idea why?"

"I expect it has to do with his shameful complaints."

"About me, no doubt."

She nodded uncomfortably.

"Did you know that Bishop Graham is in change of internal affairs? A nasty job, if you ask me." Rosemary said.

"No, I didn't."

She showed him a recent photo of Graham blessing a new Catholic parish in the Bronx.

"He looks way too young to be a bishop," Callahan noted.

"Thirty-five years young. He's been on the church's fast track and has a talent for getting defunct parishes out of financial ruin."

"Really?"

"Yes. The word is that he majored in finance at Cornell University, and he even worked on Wall Street," she said with pride — having gained most of her information from the rectory housekeepers' gossip mill and the weekly diocesan newspapers.

"I am impressed," Callahan said.

The fact Bishop Graham had been a man of the world, young and smart, lifted his spirits. Still, he worried about the insane lies Alex had no doubt contrived against him, and he dreaded his meeting with the bishop.

Bishop Graham opened the office door.

"Please come in. I need to speak with you."

He opened the window wide and hurriedly pulled back the drapes, his lungs desperate for fresh air. Father Callahan took a chair near the window, keeping his distance from Alex. The fact he had to defend himself to the bishop was infuriating.

Bishop Graham cleared his throat, ignoring pleasantries, and got to the issue at hand.

"Father Alex has presented me with an endless list of grievances against you. Please review his letters and journals."

He slid them across the desk to Callahan. Alex sat on the edge of his chair, watching Callahan like a vulture, exhilarated when Callahan slumped in his chair and his face clouded in shock.

Bishop Graham loosened his collar, sickened by the painful drama unfolding.

"Father Callahan, I expect you have something to say in your defense?" Graham inquired.

"Plenty — but to you in private."

"Please leave us, Father Alex, until I ask you to return."

"But I must be present. I must!"

"I assure you, that would be gravely unwise. Leave."

Alex went to the kitchen and stood on a stool, drawing an opened bottle of whiskey from the top kitchen shelf and taking a slug. When he stepped down, he hopped about like a kangaroo, singing, "The slug is gone. The slug is gone."

Rosemary glared at him.

"You've lost it. I can't understand why you're not ashamed of your sorry self," she said, and grabbed her purse to leave for the day. He paid her no mind. Instead he crept to the office door to press his ear against it. He strained to listen, but heard nothing — unaware he had grown half deaf.

Back in the office, Father Callahan slammed Alex's journals on the desk.

"These are embarrassing, despicable lies." He rubbed the spot in his neck that was throbbing in pain. "Alex is a raging alcoholic. He's lost his marbles. He hasn't preached a sermon in years. He lives in the Dark Ages. He doesn't give a damn about his parishioners, let alone church business," his voice cracked angrily. "I've been forbidden to say public Mass, or preach except to hear confessions. What in God's name is the use of defending myself? You'll believe what you will."

"Father," the bishop said in a level voice, "that's exactly what I intend to do. In this situation I have no problem believing your side of the story."

He took the journals and letters and tore them to shreds, tossing them into the wastebasket.

"Before I leave I will inform Father Alex that you are to preach on Sundays, and that the altar is to face the people, and the Mass to be said in English. You can continue to employ and house the janitor, and keep your little dog."

Father Callahan relaxed a bit, but sweat was dripping down his back in buckets.

"Lest I forget to mention this matter," the bishop continued, "Father Alex has a lot to say about your so-called relationship with a Bernice White."

Father Callahan cast his gaze out the window. Given the chance, he would twist the living daylights out of Alex.

"Preposterous," he growled, too upset to utter another word.

Bishop Graham rubbed his fingers thoughtfully on the gold-chained cross that hung low on his neck.

"I've often been tempted to turn this parish over to the Franciscans, given how dysfunctional it's been." He loosened his collar, which had stuck to his neck in the heat of the room.

"If you don't mind, I'd appreciate a glass of ice water."

"Of course," Callahan replied, and he hurried out the office, startling Alex, who was plastered against the office door. Callahan pushed him to the wall as he continued on.

Bishop Graham allowed the ice water to trickle slowly down his parched throat, enjoying the brief respite from dealing with this mess. He opened a file of confidential papers from his briefcase, and when he did, a letter slid to the floor. Before Graham could snatch it, Callahan scooped it up, his eyes glued to a yellow highlighted page. A rush of heat rose up his neck, covering his face.

"On my life, I swear to God I don't believe this."

"I regret that you have seen it," Bishop Graham said, heaving a ragged sigh.

"Christ, Abbot Jules said I couldn't be trusted in matters of doctrine, or to be in the company of women. Look here," and he pointed to the highlighted words in large caps: *Place Father John in a ghetto parish. If he fails to measure up, take immediate action for his excommunication.*

"Unbelievable," Callahan yelled, clenching his fists. "He has no basis for distrusting and punishing me."

Bishop Graham put the letter back in its folder and into his briefcase, zipping it up. He had studied Father Callahan's personnel records and was dismayed that he had been exposed to those appalling revelations, and to Father Alex's trumped-up accusations.

"Please understand, Father," Graham said, "in my position as Vicar General I am required to know the background and complaints rendered against our priests, and to deal with them as best I can. I suspect your abbot probably had a bad case of jealousy toward you. Saints are few, even among austere monastics," he added thoughtfully.

"Nonetheless, I am impressed with your history. None of our priests have graduated from Oxford, or have been high school principals — teaching physics, no less — or a widower and then a monk-priest. Remarkable indeed," he said, smiling lightly.

"We all have histories," Callahan said, dejectedly trying to control his fury over the abbot's statements.

"My predecessor, Bishop O'Malley, was a very sick man. He should never have placed you in this parish. Worse yet, you've been forced to deal with Father Alex, who's gone off the deep end, and with your abbot's bizarre allegations. I have other fine parishes that would benefit from your experience," he said. "I'll support you, no matter what decision you make."

Father Callahan said, with enormous effort, "I want to remain here." He had grown more determined than ever not to give in to Father Alex's vindictiveness.

The bishop studied him, slightly shocked, then downed the rest of his ice water.

"Given your background, you should consider that the Greek Orthodox and the Episcopalians are open to marriage in their priesthood. It is a reasonable option if you'd be inclined toward marriage in the future."

Father Callahan's face grew hot again.

"Do you think I am incapable of handling the challenges of celibacy?"

"Celibacy is always a choice. Without options, we become desperate. I would think a once-married man might find celibacy far more challenging, since you no longer have the fortification of the cloistered monastic life."

"I suppose," he said, embarrassed that Bishop Graham felt the need to address this sensitive issue.

"From my experience, too many unscrupulous and so-called pious women are strongly attracted to handsome, charming priests such as yourself," the bishop added with a boyish grin.

Callahan had taken note that Bishop Graham was himself a very youthful, handsome and charming man just a couple of years older than himself. The thought of Bernice flashed in his mind.

"I was told you had a full life yourself before entering the priesthood," Callahan inquired.

Bishop Graham tossed his head back, laughing.

"I'll admit that in my wild days I lived high on the hog, made a ton of money on Wall Street, and lived with Rachel, my second fiancée, in a Fifth Avenue penthouse. Not to mention, I was a wayward Catholic and hadn't gone to church since first grade."

Father Callahan laughed heartily, delighted that Bishop Graham felt comfortable enough to disclose his past. He straightened up in his chair.

"What was it that changed your life?" he asked.

"On a long weekend I attended a Jesuit retreat with my girlfriend. During that retreat I experienced an epiphany of grace and saw clearly the folly of my life, which was racing out of control. It was then that I made the decision to give my life to God. In my case I felt it was a miracle."

"Then there is hope for me," Callahan said, smiling.

"Truth be told, you're the only one I've cared to tell about my naughty past," he said, laughing.

Both men were quiet for a while. Callahan wondered if celibacy was a challenge for the bishop. He realized that Bishop Graham had shared his experience to give him counsel and consolation.

"I appreciate your kindness," he said.

Bishop Graham took a business card with his private phone number from his suit pocket and placed it in Callahan's hands. "Feel free to call me at any time."

Then Graham's face hardened as he said, "Now . . . please tell Father Alex to come back to the office."

CHAPTER 16

Alex entered the office with a slight jig in his step. Bishop Graham took notice and shoved his chair further from the desk, trying to shield himself from Alex's body odor.

"When is Father Callahan being excommunicated and sent back to Ireland?" Alex asked, unable to control his excitement.

"I don't intend to do any such thing. Sit down and pay close attention to every damn word I say."

Father Alex sank into his chair, shaken by the bishop's tone.

"Father, you've lost your way. God only knows why, or for how long. You stink like a dead fish. Here's the phone number for Dr. Ralph Rosen, a top psychiatrist at Beacon Sanatorium. He'll put you on a detox and rehab program. Call him after I leave."

"I'm perfectly fine. I don't even drink," Alex insisted.

"You're dealing with me now, not sick old Bishop O'Malley — God rest his soul," Graham replied. "If you don't get off the booze, I'll drag you to the city drunk tank myself. Believe me, it won't be pretty."

Father Alex glared at him.

"I'm a kind, hard-working priest, and you have a nasty temper," he snorted.

"You've yet to experience the extent of my temper." Graham rose to his feet and slammed his briefcase on the desk, shocked at Alex's delusionary state of mind. "Father Callahan is to say public Mass, preach on Sundays, keep his dog and do whatever the hell else he wants to improve this dysfunctional church. Do you understand me?"

"But —"

"Don't *but* me. Look at these piles of bills, none opened. Look at these letters from parishioners and children. Can you possibly explain yourself?"

"The church doesn't have enough money to pay all the bills, and I work myself to the bone."

Graham laughed bitterly.

"Working yourself to the bone? Listening all day to that damned television, hiding in your infested room? The archdiocese has been subsidizing this hole of a church for years, thanks largely to your lousy administration.

"You don't give Sunday sermons, you're always late, and nothing is going on at this church except confessions and the greenhouse. Why don't you eat in the dining room with Father Callahan?"

"He's insubordinate. He treats me with disrespect, that's why."

"Only disrespect? Consider yourself one lucky man. I was informed you desecrated his personal possessions, that you took his wedding rings. Christ, the life you live is a disgrace to your priesthood."

Father Alex hung his head, faking contriteness, but silently fuming.

"And throw your stinky slippers and dirty clothes into the trash. You look and smell like a rat-infested cesspool. Go to your room, shave, and rinse out your whiskey mouth. Do you have a tub?"

Alex nodded.

"Good. Soak your stinky body with a ton of soap." Graham rose angrily from his chair. "Count on my return very soon. If you have a brain left in that sick head of yours, I'll expect you to be on the mend by then," he said, though he seriously doubted that Alex would change at all.

Father Alex shuffled out of the office, muttering a litany of objections that the bishop could hear easily.

Saddened, Bishop Graham picked up his briefcase, and Father Callahan walked him to his car.

"Thank you for your encouragement," he said simply.

"My visit has been long overdue. I'm sorry for what you've had to go through today. God's peace be with you." He got into his car and drove off.

* * *

As he drove, Graham gave serious thought to Father Callahan's potential. He sensed that under his mentorship, with his help in navigating through church politics, Callahan could perhaps rise through the ranks of the church as quickly as he had done.

"Perhaps" was the million-dollar question. When he thought again of his confrontation with Father Alex, he opened a package of peppermint mints, grinding them between his teeth.

* * *

Father Alex's lies and Abbot Jules' condemnations had shaken Callahan to his core. He questioned if he had been running from life after his wife's tragic death by becoming a priest and a monk. Bishop Graham's advice that people needed options lest they despair made sense. Absolutely. The fact Bishop Graham had been so surprisingly candid with him gave him hope.

He returned to the church sacristy and locked the door, stripped off his shirt and gazed in the side mirror at the dragon tattoo on his back. He reached his left arm around to his back, gently caressing her long black beak.

"For many a moon I've loved you," he said in a broken voice. He rested deep in the armchair, stretched out his legs and closed his eyes, letting his mind drift to boyhood memories . . .

* * *

Pete O'Connor, a renowned artist and sculptor in Dublin, did not look kindly at the disheveled eighteen-year-old who entered his studio while he was hard at work.

"What brings you here?" he said, no welcome in his tone.

"I've been looking at your paintings in the window. Really nice work you do."

O'Connor softened a shade.

The teenager moved to the sparkling-black marble bust of a woman, veiled with her head bowed.

"Beautiful," Callahan said. The hand he reached out to touch its gleaming surface was slapped away immediately.

"Don't touch, laddie!" O'Connor scolded. "It's off to the Metropolitan Museum of Art in New York City tomorrow, as I will be."

"It looks so real. Did you have a model?"

O'Connor wiped the statue's face with a soft cloth as tenderly as he would a child's.

"Yes. For weeks I had been looking for the perfect model. Eventually I discovered a young, beautiful nun attending Dublin University. With some persuasion, she agreed to pose for me. Now be gone, laddie. I have work to do."

Callahan did not move an inch. "I've heard you're a master ink artist."

"Who told you that?"

"Vincent O'Brian."

"I rarely do tattoos any more these days. A kid like you can't afford me anyhow."

"How much?"

"One thousand pounds," O'Connor snickered.

The teenager stood his ground, hard in thought, his heels dug in deep.

"I'm curious," O'Connor said, leaning against his worktable, "what dreams have you for a tattoo?"

"I want a Celtic dragon with Ireland's green and yellow colors. I want it to cover my chest, fiery flames out of its mouth, and to be female — with a bit of kindness in her eyes."

"A female dragon with kind eyes? Laddie, it's a fierce male dragon you want. And forget kind eyes on such a wild beast. I fear you be touched in the head!"

The artist pounded the table and howled with laughter so hard he could hardly stand.

"In all respect, sir, the female is more fierce, defends her young. I want love to show in her eyes—that's what I want," Callahan said, his fists balled tight against his sides.

"I don't like dragons or their strange mythology; nothin' about those hideous creatures inspires me."

"I feel you'll love her as I do," the teen insisted.

O'Connor shook his head, a look of pity crossing his face.

"Be gone, laddie. Don't come back unless you have the money, and best not steal it. I'd find someone else if I were you."

"No one good as you," the younger man said.

"At least we agree on something. One more thing. Lassies won't feel romantic when they look into the face of that ugly dragon on your chest, so better to have it on your back."

He waved Callahan out, sure he would never return, and lifted his sculpture into a wooden crate.

Now the teenager was desperate to get a thousand pounds. It took him seven months of playing poker in seedy back rooms of bars, but he did it. Each night he silently thanked his departed grandfather, a champion poker player who had taught him well.

On a Saturday afternoon in early spring the young man burst into O'Connor's studio.

"Remember me?" he asked.

The artist stared, dumbfounded.

"On my mother's dear grave, I never thought you'd be back."

But Callahan had a paper bag full of money and spilled the cash out onto the artist's wooden worktable, then took his sweet time counting it out.

"Got to hand it to you, laddie, you are a surprise," O'Connor said, and led the younger man to a dark, windowless room at the back of his studio. He turned on a fiercely bright light.

"Are you prepared for the pain you will feel once I get started with the needle, putting that tattoo on your back?"

"How much pain?"

"From the looks of your back, more than a lot."

Taken aback, the teen assumed O'Connor was trying to scare him, giving him a chance to back down.

"I can handle it," Callahan said, convinced the artist was bluffing.

"I don't want to do tattoos any longer and I don't really know why I've agreed to do this one for you, laddie. But you must promise not to tell a soul — dead or alive — who's done it."

"I promise."

"Lie on your stomach."

So Callahan laid flat on his stomach for hours, tears rolling down his face. When he begged for a break, it didn't matter to O'Connor.

"Grow up," he said. So Callahan clenched his teeth, and the artist kept going.

Several times Callahan thought he would pass out — and he may have. Looking back, he was never sure.

When O'Connor proclaimed himself done, he walked Callahan over to a full-length mirror on the wall and handed him a glass of water. The young man's face clearly showed that he was overcome with the dragon's wild ferocity and astonishing beauty.

O'Connor gave him a fatherly pat on the head.

"Good luck to you, John Callahan, and don't come back. I'll create no more tattoos in my day."

Through the window of his studio the artist watched Callahan do a wild, crazy dance in the street. Callahan could hear O'Connor laughing and clapping exuberantly. That night he also discovered that O'Connor had returned his thousand pounds, rubber-banded in a neat bundle in his jacket pocket.

Far beyond the staggering skill displayed in the tattoo, it was O'Connor's kindness toward a wild young kid that still touched Callahan, all these years later. For years his dragon had been the armament he needed, but now he wondered whether he was in urgent need for more. Would he choose a woman — and his old life — or would he increase his commitment to God, and to celibacy?

CHAPTER 17

Wednesday lunches had become a regular gathering at the rectory for Rosemary, Derrick, Bernice, Callahan and Casey, whom Callahan had coaxed into joining them as a way to take the detective's mind at least briefly away from the pain and frustration of his stalled investigation.

Gradually Callahan had grown a bit more comfortable around Bernice, though he still refused to sit next to her if he could possibly avoid it. Rosemary had taken to Bernice even more, however.

With Father Callahan's approval, Bernice had renovated the rectory's first floor. A new round oak dining table with soft emerald-cushioned chairs graced the dining room, allowing everyone to converse with each other comfortably. The threadbare carpets had been replaced with bright oak flooring.

Rosemary was so taken with the new kitchen that she often moved her fingers over the smooth surfaces of its ivory cupboards. Cherry furniture and comfortable cream-colored sofas were a welcome sight in the living room.

The two downstairs bedrooms had new queen-size beds, walnut dressers, new showers and large tubs fit for a king. Walls painted in a light almond color throughout the first floor were calming to the eye. Callahan was delighted with the renovation, and he didn't give a damn about the condemnations and complaints from Alex, who still lived like a drunken hermit in his filthy upstairs bedroom.

Today Alex had opened his bedroom door and listened to the downstairs conversation, resentful and angry. He kicked his dirty slippers against his bedroom wall, which was yellowed from his chain-smoking.

Rosemary had set a large plate of hot dogs and buns on the table and joined them. Derrick and Casey laughed and joked, licking mustard from their sticky fingers and dropping a ton of crumbs on the floor. Woofy lapped them up as fast as they fell and then returned to perch herself close to Derrick's shoes, since he usually dropped the most.

Derrick enjoyed getting a rise out of Bernice, so he said playfully, "Take a look at those long nails. Related to Dracula, by chance?"

"Well, pretty boy," she retorted with a wink at the disheveled janitor, "it looks like you need a whole lot more than just a manicure."

Casey usually came early for lunch and stayed late, and he always tried to eat his dessert before Derrick did, since he felt that the young custodian would gobble more than his fair share. Rosemary soon realized she was cooking more than twice as much as usual for Wednesday lunches to satisfy Casey's and Derrick's incredible appetites.

After lunch Father Callahan pushed back from the table with an unusual sense of wellbeing. He had come to enjoy these "family" lunches and, all things considered, the past few days had been unusually calm. Then Rosemary placed a pile of mail on the table next to him. Surprised, he opened a letter from Robin.

Dear Father,

I am renting a cozy house in Somerville, N.J. near my aunt's home and taking nursing classes. I've been working as a waitress in my aunt's restaurant at the country club. The tips are amazing. I met Justin, a wonderful guy. He owns his own electronics business and does real well. He's Catholic. Bet you won't believe this, but I'm taking convert classes. We are engaged to be married this summer. Been so happy, think of you often.

Robin.

His spirits rose. He felt he truly had done some good. He perched her letter where he could see it, on top of his dresser by his small statue of Saint Francis of Assisi. For a second he wondered about Heckler, Robin's abuser. Would Callahan have beaten him further, even killed him, if he were not a priest? He struggled with his conscience, but visualizing the scene gave him more of a rush than ten cups of coffee.

At 2 a.m. the phone rang. Half awake, he reached for it on his side table and tumbled to the floor. As he crawled and groped to find it, it seemed to ring louder and louder.

"Hello," he mumbled.

"This is Dr. Peters at New York Presbyterian Hospital's emergency room. I have a patient, Sheila Haines, who is in terrible shape. She has been crying and asking for you but, frankly, it's touch and go whether she makes it. Any chance you can get here?"

"My God! I'm on my way."

He fumbled for his clothes and sped through the early-morning city. The ER waiting room was quiet except for a man who was talking loudly to himself.

He approached the admitting nurse.

"Dr. Peters just phoned me about a patient, Sheila Haines?"

"Yes, we've been expecting you." She buzzed the door open and pointed. "Follow the yellow line. She's in Room H."

Then she paused.

"I regret to have to say this, but if there's a white sheet over her face, she has expired."

He raced down the long hall, dread washing through him, and pulled back the curtains to stare at Sheila, who had a thin white sheet covering her body — but not her face.

"Thank God," he said out loud.

Two nurses were monitoring the flow of blood and other fluids dripping into her through long intravenous tubes.

He stopped and caught his breath.

Checking Sheila's vital signs was a baby-faced doctor spouting directions to the nurses. Callahan walked to the far corner of the room and leaned heavily against the white wall, weak-kneed, unable to think straight.

Ten minutes passed until the doctor led him out of the room and spoke softly.

"I am Dr. Peters. Thank you for coming. Ms. Haines was admitted here forty minutes before I called you, bleeding to death from a horrific botched abortion. We're flooding her body with blood and antibiotics. Underground abortionists kill more women than I dare count," he spat out.

"Will she make it?" the priest asked, feeling his gut grow tight.

Dr. Peters made a small smile.

"In your holy world, Father, you may need to find a big-time miracle. She's barely conscious. Speak to her before it's too late. She may or may not respond, but hurry."

Dr. Peters turned to attend to a gunshot victim who was screaming at the top of his lungs in the next room. The priest heard the doctor snarl, "Don't tell me, Tony, you're back for the third time."

"A fine place to meet," Callahan said gently as he held Sheila's ice-cold hand. Her eyes flickered a slit as she struggled to speak.

"Should have . . . have listened to you," she labored to whisper. "Hudson promised me paradise. Took me to a depraved doctor . . . near killed me." She gasped and tears streamed down her pale cheeks.

"We all make mistakes," he said in a desperate attempt to console her. "I'm going to give you a special blessing to make you well." In his rush to leave the rectory he had forgotten his prayer book and the holy oils that were used to minister to the dying.

"I bless you in the name of the Father, and of the Son and of the Holy Spirit," he prayed, touching her forehead like a feather. After his prayer ritual, a faint lift of color rose on her face. "You're a tough lassie. I swear to Almighty God you are going to pull through."

"I refuse to die," she said, but she spit up blood. The attending nurse wiped her mouth gently and returned to monitoring the heart machine.

"Come closer," she said, and he bent to her cheek.

"On my grandmother's grave, I vow that Glenn Hudson and this demonic doctor will regret the day they were born," she hissed.

He rubbed her hands, which had begun to warm. He knew the power of this kind of hate like he knew his own skin. It was a place where nothing on earth seemed impossible. Perhaps it would at least give her strength to recover.

"Rest easy, lassie. You're going to make it."

She closed her eyes and dozed as Dr. Peters returned to check her vitals and the heart monitor.

"Well, well. It looks like your friend has turned the corner. You do indeed seem to hold the power of miracles, Father."

"Don't think so, doctor; it's you who's done the miracle."

Dr. Peters held Sheila's medical chart loosely to his side.

"She will remain in the hospital for three or more days, depending on the rate of her recovery. I'm sending her to 44-C, a private room on the fourth floor. If you want to hang around, the cafeteria on the bottom floor is open 24/7. The food actually is quite tasty." Then he hurried off. The ER was filling quickly with suffering adults and howling children.

Callahan felt an intense need to stay at Sheila's side, so he headed to the cafeteria for breakfast. He found himself taking short breaths through his mouth, shielding himself from the mingled smell of antiseptic and stale cigarettes.

He had little appetite left by the time he reached the cafeteria, even though it displayed long counters filled with fried bacon, ham, scrambled eggs, French toast and pancakes, blending with the aroma of fresh coffee. A good number of nurses, technicians and doctors sat in tight clusters to eat and talk.

He sat alone, sipping black coffee, worried about Sheila. A place in hell was too good a place for the likes of Hudson and his doctor.

He told himself he should ponder how Jesus would handle this situation, but instead he was overcome by an avalanche of searing rage.

Not taking time to find the elevator, he fairly ran up four flights of stairs to Sheila's room, arriving just as a young nurse came out.

"May I visit Sheila Haines?" he asked.

The nurse took note of the good-looking man in gray sweats and brown sneakers.

"Are you family, a boyfriend perhaps?"

"A friend," he said lightly.

She checked her chart.

"Don't think so, mister. Only a Father Callahan is listed on her visitor's list. Sorry, but that counts you out."

"I happen to be Father Callahan," he said with a boyish grin.

"You sure don't look like a priest to me."

He handed her a card bearing his name and parish.

The nurse studied it and handed it back.

"Go right in."

Priest or not, this man might be her lover. She moved to the next patient's room, entertained by the thought.

CHAPTER 18

At 7 a.m. the hospital corridors buzzed with voices over loudspeakers calling to doctors and nurses. Adding to the noise were hospital cleaners and service workers wheeling food carts into patients' rooms. Cigarette smoke drifted through the hallways and from the hospital vents. Radios and television sets from the patients' rooms added to the din. It was not a quiet sanctuary conducive to healing.

He quietly closed the door of Sheila's room behind him. She was slightly elevated in her bed, gazing out the window into a row of concrete skyscrapers.

"Ah, lassie, it looks like you've risen from the dead," he said, delighted.

She turned painfully toward him, not lifting her head from her pillow. Her long hair was drawn back, and her white hospital gown looked strange on a woman who was given to gorgeous, sexy clothes and flashy makeup. Nonetheless, he found her to be amazingly beautiful despite her near-death experience.

"Please hold my hands — so cold. I'm cold all over."

He went to the closet and pulled out two wool blankets, tucking them tightly around her from her neck to her feet. "You're going to get toasty in no time," he said cheerfully.

He wanted to hold her to his heart and to warm her from the heat of his body, as he often had done with his baby sister Irene.

Instead he rubbed her hands until they warmed. Their relationship had been a confrontational one, so he was surprised she had turned to him in this crisis. Did she simply have no one else? He silently vowed to help her however he could, but he already doubted whether that would be enough.

In that moment he remembered how the Butler boys used to enjoy bullying Irene, seven years younger than he, until one afternoon when he was coming home from high school he spotted them pushing her off her bike and tearing off her new wool jacket.

He had pulled the eldest brother to the ground and beaten him to a pulp while the others ran. Eventually his father had wrestled him off Jimmy Butler, and the Butler boys never bothered his sister again. He wondered if it was in his blood somehow, this need to protect all women as he had his sister, his wife, and now Robin and even Sheila.

"Would you care for some water?" he asked.

She nodded. He filled a small paper cup and held it to her lips. She sipped it slowly.

"I hope you're not in a hurry to leave," she said anxiously.

"I have plenty of time for you, lassie," he said, feeling remorse for his harshness in the confessional.

She looked so frail and vulnerable as she slipped deeper into the hospital bed in sleep. He took the stairs to the lobby's first-floor gift shop and looked at the magazines, books, flowers, stuffed toys and candy. In the far corner he spotted a vase of yellow and white daisies with a soft brown teddy bear squeezed against it.

"This is perfect," he said to the cashier.

He placed the flowers on the table in front of Sheila and tucked the lifelike teddy bear into the blankets near her hands. Exhausted, he sank low in the recliner, leaning back and joining Sheila in slumber.

A nurse had come into the room. She took note of the young woman and man, both strikingly beautiful in sleep. It was a tender sight with the teddy bear near Sheila's hands. She knew the man had been with her for hours, and was moved by his devotion.

"No better medicine," she whispered softly and left the room happier than when she had come in.

When he woke, Sheila was still asleep. He sang softly his favorite chorus from "The Ferryman."

"Where the strawberry beds sweep down to the Liffy, you kissed away the worries from my brow. I love you well today, and I'll love you more tomorrow. If you ever loved me, Molly, love me now."

She had woken but pretended to be asleep while she listened to the tender love in his voice, wishing she had met someone like him to adore and cherish instead of that cruel, heartless Hudson — who had discarded her like rubbish.

"Ah, lassie, you're awake?"

He moved closer to her side. She opened her eyes wide, felt the teddy bear by her hands and saw the cheerful daisies with their delicate heads bent toward her in greeting.

"You could have left, but you stayed. You've lavished me with gifts, and mostly with love," she said through her tears.

"I'm just an old softie," he teased.

"Not close to old, but a dear softie for sure."

"Children like naming their stuffed animals. What will you name your teddy bear?"

She smiled broadly.

"I'll name my teddy 'Care.' He'll be my Care Bear.

"I don't understand your kindness," she said. "My life has no dignity. I am headstrong and arrogant. I disrespected your advice and nearly got myself killed."

"I'm the last person on earth to judge you or anyone, and I pray God will not judge my life."

She tried to rise higher in the hospital bed. Quickly he lifted her to an upright position. "I was on death's door," she said, searching his face.

"Almost, lassie, but amazingly you're alive."

Dr. Peters entered the room to review her medical chart, and a wide smile broke out on his face.

"I thought you'd be off your shift by now and at home snoring," Father Callahan quipped.

"Not close. I wanted to check on Sheila here, to be sure she was still with us," he teased lightly. "Keep up this remarkable progress and you'll be out of here in two days." He noticed the flowers and the little teddy tucked in her hands. "Looks like someone cares for you."

When the doctor left her room he grabbed a food cart, dancing around it and singing, *Stayin' Alive. Stayin' Alive. Whether you're a brother, whether you're a mother, you're stayin' alive, stayin' alive,"* then regained his composure before strolling to the nurse's station — where doctors and nurses clapped and laughed.

Father Callahan had also been watching him. He asked a passing nurse, "Does Dr. Peters do that often?"

"It depends on his mood. He happens to be the youngest doctor on staff, turned 27 yesterday, kind of a kid still," she said, then moved down the hall.

He returned to Sheila.

"You've been a good friend," she said, choking up. "I have no family in the states, and no real friends, given my line of work."

He didn't feel he was much of a true friend, but after a pause he asked, "If you are so inclined, tell me how you ended up here."

She lowered her head, unable to look him in the eye.

"Yesterday morning Hudson took me to a horrific doctor in the Bronx for an abortion. The place was dirty and dilapidated. I wanted to leave desperately, but Hudson convinced me I'd be fine, and he'd pick me up and take me home right after the abortion. He promised to file for divorce that day, and drove off before I could change my mind.

"I was alone and so terrified. This Dr. Burns had no nurse. From the way he examined my breasts I knew I was in trouble. He gave me a shot to put me under. I forced myself to stay awake. I could fell his fingers inside me, but not like a doctor. I couldn't scream. I couldn't move my arms or legs, and then I felt him raping me. When I tried to yell, he gave me another shot."

Callahan dug his hands into the bed rail.

"After the abortion, Hudson wasn't in the waiting room like he promised. I told the doctor I felt I was bleeding too much. He shrugged it off, said it was normal.

"I had to take a cab home. All day I tried to get a hold of Hudson. They told me he was in meetings. That evening I was bleeding like a faucet, called 9-1-1 and was taken to the ER. Hudson lied to me. He never loved me. He almost got me killed. I despise him."

"The good news, lassie, is you're on the mend and you'll be home soon."

"Hudson is a dead man — and his rotten doctor," she said through gritted teeth.

"Metaphorically?" he asked.

"There are many ways to suffer and many ways to die," she hissed, looking past him. He had no trouble agreeing with that.

"Please focus on getting your health back. Call me for anything at any time," he said earnestly. "By the way," he added casually, "do you remember the location of that doctor's office?"

"Five-eighteen Stone Street, in the rotten part of the Bronx. On my life, I'll never forget that dump."

"I'll come by tomorrow." Her eyelids had grown heavy. "Sleep, lassie." He lowered her bed from its upright position.

Late that afternoon Sheila buzzed the nurse.

"Please help me get me up. I want to walk up and down the hall."

She was determined to regain her full strength as quickly as possible. She pushed herself out of bed, determined to destroy Glenn Hudson and Dr. Burns.

CHAPTER 19

He drove to the office of Dr. Burns in the seedy section of the Bronx and parked his car two blocks away. Many of the dilapidated apartment buildings were abandoned, and the street was eerily quiet for a late afternoon, except for an alley cat scratching its mangy back against a broken Dumpster.

He walked up two rickety steps to a gray peeling door marked 13-B and listened for activity but heard none. He strolled across the street, leaning against a mailbox, his eyes fastened on the door. From time to time he glanced at his watch, wondering if the creep was in there.

Digging his hands into his pockets he told himself, "I'll just confront him, that's all it's going to be." No one had come in or left the building for the past hour. As he was about to give up, a short, pudgy, balding, middle-aged man emerged, locking his office door.

A rush of rage swept through Callahan as he followed Burns to a gray Buick convertible. An instinct warned Callahan to leave. He turned back in the direction of his car, until in his mind's eye he saw Sheila's limp body in the ER, then turned again and hurried after Burns.

When the doctor opened his car door, Callahan grabbed his left shoulder.

"Burns?"

"Yeah. Who the hell are you?" trying to squeeze out of Callahan's iron grip.

"Know Sheila Haines?"

"Never heard of her. Take your hands off me."

"You raped her. She nearly bled to death from your infectious abortion."

He struggled in vain to get loose. Callahan's hand held Burns' shoulder like a vise.

"I swear I don't know any so-called Sheila."

"She was at your office two days ago. She was brought by a man who called himself Dover. He paid you five hundred dollars in cash for her abortion," twisting his arm painfully behind his back.

"You got the wrong person."

He hurled Burns against the car's front door, broke both his hands and some fingers, then kicked his car keys far under the car and walked off without hurry.

"Someone help me," Burns screamed, but his cries fell from the air like dying wasps.

Callahan returned to the rectory, exhilarated. In Belfast he had done worse and loved it. Burns' life as he had lived it was over, for damned sure. No more women would suffer as Sheila had.

That night he slept like a baby.

* * *

For two days Sheila walked the halls of the hospital. When no one was watching, she went up and down the exit stairs, pushing herself to regain the fullness of her strength, driven by hatred and revenge toward Burns and Hudson.

Friday morning Sheila waited by her hospital room's window for Dr. Peters' arrival to discharge her. She was dressed in a shimmering emerald silk dress and black high heels delivered from B. Altman & Company of Fifth Avenue. Her glossy blond hair reached to the middle of her back, and brilliant ruby lipstick exalted the beauty of her face and her large blue eyes, dazzling in the sunlight streaming through the window.

Dr. Peters' head was bowed as he came into the room reviewing her medical chart. He stopped short, taken aback by the gorgeous woman standing before him. "My God," he blurted. "You look . . . beautiful," dropping his chart on the floor.

Sheila laughed, amused.

"How are you feeling?" he asked, sheepishly picking up his chart.

"Quite well, thanks to you," her lips curled in a sweet smile.

"Wonderful," he said. "I do admit I hardly recognized you," placing a bottle of antibiotics in her hand. "You must continue taking this medication for six more days. If you don't, you will be back in the ER and none of us will be smiling.

"Please sit down," he added. "I need to discuss some good and bad news."

She tensed. "A problem?"

"That depends. Quite honestly I can't believe you're alive. You suffered extensive damage to your internal organs from the infection and abortion. You would have bled to death, had you not come in when you did."

He paused.

"Presently you have less than a fifty-fifty chance to have children."

"But I'm only twenty-six," she whimpered, her lips drawn tight.

"In your case that could be a plus. Still, no guarantees."

He looked at her squarely.

"I have made an appointment this Friday for you to see Dr. Winston, the best gynecologist in New York. I've spoken to her about your condition. Promise me that you'll see her, and no sex for at least three months."

"I promise." *No sex for months — what a relief*, she thought.

"You saved my life, doctor. I can never thank you enough," she said, and planted a soft kiss on his forehead.

"That's what I do," he said, a boyish grin playing on his hot face.

The nurse wheeled her down the hall to the front entrance of the hospital. A smart young driver wearing a black suit and gold tie helped her into a town car, helping her into the back seat.

She closed her eyes, vowing never to return to the cries of the hospital's suffering that were still echoing in her head. She cuddled Care, her teddy, feeling he understood the inner workings of her heart. It didn't matter that he was just a stuffed bear.

Her doorman, dressed in a classy black uniform, carried her roses through the elegant Park Avenue lobby. Plush scarlet carpets led to a shiny brass elevator. She pressed the button, ecstatic to be back in her penthouse suite with its sweeping views of the city lights.

Carefully she placed her flowers in an imported crystal vase on a mahogany table in the living room and tucked precious Care onto her bedroom's white satin pillow, kissing him.

She opened all the windows in her apartment, welcoming in the cool breeze to freshen her room. The room was elegantly furnished from Italy, the home of her mother's family. Still, she was obsessed with Hudson and Burns.

She fingered the files in her immaculate home office and found the phone number of Antonio, a third cousin through marriage on her mother's side. She dialed his number in Tuscany, Italy, tapping her fingers anxiously on her spotless mahogany desk.

"It's been far too long, darling, since we've chatted," he said, his voice smooth and sensual.

"I agree," she said, her nerves on end. "How is my grandmother's family?"

"Happy, fat and lazy," he said lightly. "I'm not fat or lazy, and I'd be happier if I had you in my bed, honey child," he chuckled.

"That would be fun," she thought, briefly.

She had met him after her grandmother's funeral in White Plains, New York, at a rather lively gathering of family from Italy. She had watched him move among the mourners, heart-stopping handsome, kissing women's hands like an older gentleman.

"Who is he?" she had asked her uncle, pointing in his direction.

"Antonio Mancini, one of your cousins."

"How old is he?"

"Twenty-one."

Antonio had been watching her as well, and he approached her as she sat alone in the far corner of the living room.

"Care to take a garden stroll?" he coaxed, smiling. Before she could answer, he had taken her hand and led her to the rose gardens behind the house.

She was just fifteen, but her face and figure made her seem much older. He lifted her chin and began kissing her. They kissed again and again until he took her to a secluded area, pulled up her dress, aroused her in maddening ways and pushed himself inside her willing body.

Soon they heard their Aunt Helen calling him.

"I must see what she wants," he said huskily, leaving the young girl alone in the garden, no longer a virgin. Hours later he came to her as she was cleaning dishes in the kitchen.

"Come with me to my apartment," he whispered, but their Aunt Helen saw them knitted together.

"What are you doing, Antonio? Sheila's but a child. Find someone your own age."

"How old are you?" he asked.

"Fifteen," she whispered.

"Christ," he blurted, and moved away in shock.

Sheila smiled at these memories but pushed them aside.

"What has ruffled your feathers, darling?" Antonio asked. "You sound upset."

Through bouts of sobs, she told him about Hudson's deception, Burns' rape and the botched, infectious abortion, and Father Callahan's loving care. He listened, heartsick, remembering as he did every time they spoke how he had fallen in love with her.

"Honey, I gave up that business years ago," he said, "but given your situation I will help you. Be patient. I'll get back to you in a few days."

She filled her bathtub with steaming water and eased in slowly, until she completely relaxed. She had no doubt that Antonio would take care of the situation to her complete satisfaction, and that brought a smile to her lips.

CHAPTER 20

At 1 p.m. Casey sauntered toward the greenhouse where Father Callahan chatted with church volunteers. "Hey, Padre, got a sec?"

"Depends," he said with a grin. Sheila had just phoned, lifting his mood.

"I'm on the mend," she had said. "I plan to visit my cousin Antonio in Tuscany in a few weeks, and begin a new life in Italy. My two apartments are in escrow."

"A new life! Nothing can be better. But before you leave, I would like to see you."

"I promise," she said cheerfully.

For a fleeting moment he thought how he had crushed Burns' hands and fingers. The memory gave him a surge of adrenaline and, somehow, no trace of regret.

"How about coming to my place?" Casey was asking, pulling him back from his thoughts. "I want to show you something."

"A change of pace will suit me fine," and he jumped into the front seat of Casey's immaculate but sputtering old truck. He found the seat was bone-hard to the butt.

Casey drove to his home, tucked in a cozy middle-class neighborhood of Queens across from a small park, where mothers pushed their children back and forth in worn swings. Toddlers played in sandboxes with dogs tugging at their shoes; it was a park filled with laughter and innocence.

"Bet you enjoy living across from this kids' park."

"Yeah. But usually I can't squeeze a drip of time to enjoy it," Casey grumbled.

Casey ushered him into his small one-story house. Outside, golden autumn leaves from the maple tree that graced the front lawn lay scattered over tall grass. Inside, piles of papers and files cluttered the gray-carpeted floors and the large glass coffee table.

"Looks like you're in need of a housekeeper, and most definitely a secretary," Callahan said. "If you don't mind, how about getting some fresh air in here? Don't take me wrong, Casey, but your house smells like a sick chimney."

"Oh, yeah," the detective said sheepishly as he opened all the windows, allowing freshness to push through the lace curtains. "My pad used to be tidy before Chief Duffy dumped all his work on me to worm through.

"He's so damned paranoid, I can't even sneak in the back door of the precinct; he swears dirty cops hide in the cracks of the floor." He blew his nose like a foghorn.

"Coffee?"

Callahan went to the kitchen, stacked with dirty dishes that were threatening to fall over the sink's porcelain edge.

"No thanks."

Casey shrugged. "Maybe I will get someone in here to clean up — know anyone up to the job?"

"Rosemary might. Whoever it's going to be has to be tough of skin," Callahan said as he eased himself out of the kitchen. He noticed a plant drooping on the window ledge, so he found a cup and drenched the ailing plant with lukewarm water. In short time, its leaves lifted in gratitude.

In that moment Casey wondered if it had been wise to invite the padre into his junkyard, but he let it slide.

"Chief Ford contacted me yesterday, reminded me that his daughter's diamond ruby ring — You remember, the one valued at $20,000 that he gave her for her twenty-first birthday? — was missing from Karen's jewel case. He wanted to know what I knew about it.

"This morning I went over to Abraham & Strauss jewelry store, and they gave me a catalog of their Victoria jewel collection and a picture of the missing ring.

"Here, take a look."

"Breathtaking . . . beautiful," Callahan said.

"Bet this fuck took it as a trophy," Casey said, massaging his earlobe.

"I have a feeling he took the ring to a pawnshop to get his infected claws on some cash," Callahan replied.

Casey nodded at the possibility, stepping gingerly over the scattered papers on the floor.

"I know of a specific pawnshop in Chinatown on Mott Street. It's in the back room of The Dragon restaurant. They specialize in posh stolen merchandise. I was in there two years ago."

Father Callahan's eyebrows twitched. "How about checking it out?"

Twenty minutes later they entered the crowded restaurant, where the heavy aroma of Chinese food greeted them.

Casey swept his tongue hungrily over his lips. "Didn't have breakfast, half starved, how about lunch?"

"Good idea," Callahan said. Casey found a small table wedged in the rear corner of the bustling restaurant where it was easy to observe people's comings and goings.

Paper lanterns hung low from the ceiling, their dim lights flickering on the ruby walls covered with golden dragon tapestry. Boyish male waiters half-ran from table to table, speaking Mandarin. Everyone in the restaurant was Chinese except them.

"Any Chinese restaurants in Ireland?"

"A few in Dublin. When I was studying at Oxford, Hui, my Chinese roommate, taught me conversational Mandarin. On Saturdays we'd frequent Chinese restaurants in London."

They ordered chow mein and wonton for starters.

"Love this food," Casey said, finishing off two heaping plates in no time.

They ate without conversation, their eyes fastened on a rotund but heavily muscled man glued against the back wall next to a heavy black curtain. Tempted to order another round of food, Casey shoved his plate back and rose, leaving a generous roll of cash on the table that was quickly snatched by their waiter.

They approached the stoic man by the curtain blocking their entry to the pawnshop. Father Callahan spoke politely to him in Mandarin. His thick tight lips lifted a notch and he pulled back the curtain, leading them down a dark, stuffy hallway. He opened the door to a dimly lit room stacked with statues, pictures, swords, golden dragons, and rows of expensive jewelry.

Guns and rifles were secured in double-locked drawers behind a short, white-bearded Chinese man who appeared to be in his sixties. He was watching them cautiously. To his left stood a buff man with his eyes set on them like a rattlesnake.

Father Callahan took the initiative and spoke to the old man in Mandarin.

"We need your help," he said in a smooth and affable tone. "My friend and I are looking for a ring," and he placed the catalog picture on the counter, sliding it in front of him.

Faintly the old man's eyes softened. The fact this stranger, though not Chinese, spoke his tongue was a matter of respect.

"I sold such a ring two weeks ago," he said in English, so softly that they leaned in closer to listen.

Casey's face brightened.

"How much did this man ask for the ring?"

"Ten thousand dollars. I gave him three thousand, sold it next day for more," his toothless smile wide.

"Did he sell you anything else?"

He turned around and pointed to a gun locked in a cabinet behind him.

Casey's neck grew hot. "May we see it?"

"Only see . . . no sell." He unlocked the cabinet and placed the revolver in front of them on the counter with his hands locked on the handle. His security man put his hand on the gun inside his jacket.

"Christ, this is a .38 Special. Cops use it," Casey said. He didn't bother asking how much he paid for it. Getting a warrant was futile. The old man would hide or sell it before they came back. In his gut he knew the old man had already sniffed him out as a cop.

"What did this man look like?" Casey asked.

He took his time responding. Tiny red veins popped out of Casey's face. He was so desperate for a break.

"Built like you," pointing to Casey, "dark glasses, told . . . take off or leave. Got mad. Took off, black eyes like coal. Brown hair. Nails . . . to stubs."

Casey knew suspect goods from suspect people found their way into such pawnshops. Chinese owners were damned sharp about what they bought, what they sold and whom they dealt with.

From the corner of his eye, Casey saw the padre linger affectionately by some statues of dragons. Christ, he spoke Mandarin, had a tattoo dragon on his back. Casey was more convinced than ever that this priest's past was a world of secrets.

Father Callahan found twelve bronze dragons caked in dirt pushed back in a shelf corner. He placed one carefully in front of the old man.

"Beautiful," he said in Mandarin, moving his fingers tenderly over the dragon's wings as if it could fly.

The shop owner watched him, pulling at his beard.

"It gives me great pleasure to buy this statue," he said in Mandarin.

"No price for you," and the old man placed it back in his hands. His security guard led them out a back door and into a stinky alley. Dumpsters overflowed with garbage, the treasured abode of well-fed rats.

"What do you think about that gun? It's a cop's gun, no doubt." Casey asked.

"Interesting," Callahan replied.

"I'm going to see if any cop guns have gone missing lately."

Casey weaved through the city traffic. The aroma of Chinese takeout filled the truck. "Now that we have a partial description of the killer, I'm going to go through a new set of mug shots," he added.

Callahan paid little attention to Casey, preoccupied with his dragon.

"It's rather sweet," pushing it toward him. "Don't you think?"

"Beauty is in the eyes of the beholder," Casey said, with no love lost for dragons. "You seemed rather comfy in that pawnshop."

"In my young days I spent a load of time in such places," and he sank low in the seat as they headed back to the rectory, closed his eyes and swept back to his young life in Belfast.

* * *

He had been easily influenced in the days of his youth. Pawnshops fascinated him. They were the home of treasures that had been purchased cheap from the hands of the hungry who desperately needed money and from the hands of criminals and thieves.

Stealing came easily to him, especially when pawnshop owners were wrangling over money at their front counters. He would move through rows of junk in Buckley's pawnshop and often help himself. One day he spotted a silver pocketknife, slipped it into his jacket pocket and walked out of the shop nonchalantly.

But Buckley grabbed his neck from behind, kicked him against the door and grabbed the pocketknife out of his jacket. Then the 225-pound bull of a man started hammering the boy with his fists.

They fought like pit bulls in knockdown, drag-out, bare-knuckle, down-and-dirty combat on the ground outside his shop. A bunch of kids gathered and began to chant, "Kill Buckley," but the shop owner banged the youth's head ferociously on the ground. Callahan nailed him in the groin and the older man doubled over, but not for long. He jumped on the boy like a bear until they heard police sirens approaching.

Buckley dragged the battered boy by his feet into his shop and locked the front door. Callahan slid against the wall, afraid every bone in his body was broken. His nose was bleeding like a fire hose, his knuckles split to the bone, his eyes swelling shut.

Buckley pulled up a chair and sat in front of him, both still panting like dogs. "Where did you learn to fight?"

"Belfast streets," Callahan panted. Buckley wiped blood from his lips with his shirtsleeve.

"You're a damned scrawny kid, but you fought tougher than most big men I know."

Callahan was hurting too much to care what the shop owner said.

"Come with me. The IRA can use a badass like you."

And Callahan did.

He learned to use a gun, ran the streets, fought like a wolverine, stole and even killed. Those were dark days in the time of The Troubles, but they were energized with danger and a cause to fight for.

Back in the rectory, he washed his new statue carefully and dried it with a soft terry cloth. When he began to examine it, he was astonished to discover tiny emeralds in its eyes, on its belly and wings.

The pawnshop keeper had to have known these jewels were precious, he thought. Could he have made a mistake? It had been discarded for God knows how long. All the similar dragons had been crusted with so much dirt, after all. Callahan struggled with his conscience. He already loved the statue but felt he had to return it, given its value.

For now, he placed it with care in front of the statue of Saint Francis of Assisi on top of his dresser. The dragon figure made him think again of Ireland.

"My past is long over — the cause, the danger, the anger, and the death."

He regarded his new dragon statue as holy somehow, and even a bit magical, offering him as much comfort and solace as hallowed prayer.

CHAPTER 21

Sheila scooped up her phone, relieved to hear Antonio's melodic voice calling from his vineyard estate in Tuscany. She leaned against the kitchen sink as rain beat like drums against the windowpane.

"How are you feeling these days, lady of my dreams?" he asked in a sensual tone.

"Stronger each day," she said hurriedly, anxious for his news.

"Wonderful," he said, relieved. "As you might expect, Burns isn't his real name. It's Shane Spencer, and he's no doctor. He was a nurse technician at Belleview Hospital for three years. Quit. Since then, been doing abortions. Has an uppity Tudor house in Long Island, no less."

"Damn!" she said.

"More news, darling — ready for it?"

"What?"

"While you were in hospital, Spencer was beat to a pulp, supposedly by street thugs, ended up in Belleview's ER, according to their reports."

She squeezed her stomach tight.

"The fingers on his right hand had to be amputated. Both his hands were broken, and his left hand has so much nerve damage he can barely use it."

"Did he report anything stolen to the police?" she asked.

"Apparently not. A rather curious situation, don't you think?"

"I guess," she said thinking hard.

"His injury occurred when you were still in hospital. Did anyone know of your situation besides hospital staff?"

"Only Father Callahan, my savior. He helped get me through my ordeal."

"Hmph! Know anything about him?"

"I remember him telling me he grew up in Belfast, became a monk in Ireland shortly after his wife's death."

"Grew up in Belfast!" Antonio chuckled quietly to himself. No doubt this man had to have been one tough thug to have punished Spencer to an inch of his life, priest or no priest. He'd give anything to meet this priest someday.

"I've learned Spencer has moved to Florida, lives with his mother, a semi-invalid. Does this satisfy you?"

"Absolutely," she said, laughing.

"I'm taking my private jet to Albany, arriving tomorrow evening. I'll take care of Glenn Hudson. Talk to you soon."

She grabbed her little Care teddy and danced around her apartment.

"Revenge is mine!" she shouted, and laughed.

Sheila had no doubt that it was Father Callahan who had come so near to killing Burns, or Spencer. He had asked for the abortion doctor's address, she recalled.

Elated at this turn of events, she made an appointment for a massage, manicure and pedicure, and wondered if perchance she would enjoy becoming a redhead.

Next evening Antonio arrived in Albany at 6 p.m. and was driven by town car to the swanky Desmond Hotel. He had stayed here often when he had visited his billionaire Uncle Ricardo, deceased five years past, a widower with no children. Antonio had inherited his vast estate of hotels worldwide and wineries in Italy, France and Napa Valley.

Antonio walked through the brick courtyard entry, admiring the hotel's colonial theme and its original oil paintings, a tribute to Colonial and American history.

Avoiding elevators, he took the stairs to the executive suite on the second floor and put the "Do Not Disturb" sign on his door. He plopped his suitcase onto the king-sized bed's velvet-gold bedspread and loaded film into his video camera and his favorite Polaroid SX-70 Sonar One Step camera.

On the cherry desk was a tall pitcher of ice water. He poured himself a generous drink, enjoyed its coolness sliding down his dry throat, and pulled back the ivory drapes to get sweeping views to the manicured rose gardens below.

He rested on the bed and watched the soccer match between Italy and England for two hours, delighted with Italy's win. At 9 p.m. he took the back stairs out of the hotel and drove off in a rented black Mercury Cougar, familiar with every corner of the city and its surrounding areas.

A well-paid source had given him detailed information about Hudson's day-to-day comings and goings, so he headed to the seedy red-light district in Rensselaer outside of Albany.

Antonio parked across from a tottering three-story apartment building, with his driver's window down, watching prostitutes in hot pants and thin tops come and go inside the apartment with their panting johns.

He waited patiently, and at 10 p.m. Saint John's Catholic Church bells tolled, as if announcing the arrival of Glenn Hudson, the corrupt attorney general of New York State.

Hudson parked his black Mercury sedan two cars in front of Antonio. He emerged, no taller than five-six, hair thinning and plain looking, wearing loose pants. Antonio scrutinized his photo. Satisfied, he sank low in the front seat.

Hudson leaned against his front fender, swinging his head back and forth until an obviously underage girl with double D boobs flounced out of the building, spotted him, crossed the street, lifted her skirt to expose her naked front, kissed him, pushed her hands into his loose pants, and rubbed him where it mattered.

They spoke loudly, the streetlight flickering on their faces.

"Come on, baby, get in my car. Let's go to the Robins Motel. It's not far from here — and more private."

"No, honey," she purred. "Gotta stay. Know how it is on Friday nights, should have gotten hold of me earlier," fluttering her eyes like a butterfly.

"Baby, I'll make it worth your while," he said, lifting her top and sucking her nipples. She took his hand and they half skipped across the street to the apartment.

Antonio followed then at a comfortable distance, his black baseball cap pulled low. They hurried up the staircase to the third floor, where squeals and moans echoed from every room.

He sauntered past the room that Hudson and the girl had gone in, and went to the fire escape balcony, balancing himself easily on the wrought-iron ledge next to their room at the far end of the building, which had no curtains.

"Perfect," he whispered to himself, and drew his still and video cameras from a light case.

Hudson, now naked and exposing a fat belly and small dick, sat on the edge of the bed smacking his lips. The nude girl wiggled her body in front of him until he grabbed her tits, moving his tongue down low on her stomach. He tossed her on the bed, pushing her legs wide apart, licking her, then pumped himself into her hot young body, and they both groaned.

Antonio worked both his cameras from every possible angle, focused and calm. Satisfied he had enough photos, he eased himself down the rickety fire escape and into the alley. Back at the hotel and famished, he ordered room service.

The hotel waiter rolled in a white linen cart loaded with a Black Angus rib roast, mashed potatoes and gravy, soft green beans with a tall-stemmed glass of Italian Piemonte red wine. It had been a rather busy day, and it was midnight when he folded himself under his bedcovers and slept soundly despite the demons yearning for vengeance.

Next morning he made three copies of the videotape and twenty-five still photos, sealing them tight in yellow envelopes. At 7 p.m., dressed in a black gabardine tuxedo with a wedding ring on his finger, intended to ward off women, he drove in a rented Bentley to the governor's mansion, a monument of history and tradition in the heart of Albany.

Throngs of guests were arriving to celebrate the visit of seven dignitaries, members of the British House of Commons. Antonio joined a group of guests showing formal invitations to the security. He flashed his forged invitation confidently and moved quickly into the reception hall, which was almost filled.

Women wore long formal gowns, flaunting expensive jewelry, and the men wore black tuxedos. He admired the Tiffany sterling silver with the New York State seal and the trumpet vases displaying white and pink lilies on white-laced linen tablecloths, and the gold-plated dishware from England.

To the side of the room an orchestra played popular music from "Evita," Chicago, and the Moody Blues. Waiters skillfully balanced their large silver trays, serving guests with an abundance of wine, encouraging them to liven up.

Antonio stood off alone, waiting until Governor Hastings was momentarily alone and then walked quickly to his side. With an air of authority he said, "Your Honor, I have urgent information for you," and pressed the yellow envelope into his hands, mouthing, "So sorry."

On the back of the envelope was scotch-taped a photo of the butt-naked Hudson straddling the young prostitute with her name, the apartment location, and the date and time.

Antonio strolled casually to the back corner of the room but remained focused on the governor, watching him hurry to a private room with his face angry and dark. Antonio was sorry to ruin the governor's evening, but it was necessary.

Inside the private room, the governor pounded his fist on the desk. Dumbfounded, he watched the video and thumbed through the photos of Hudson, his adulterous shithead attorney general.

He made a quick phone call to verify the location where Hudson had gone, a well-known red-light district. In twenty minutes Hudson was ushered into the governor's room.

"Showtime," the governor growled.

When the governor summoned Hudson, his wife decided to leave the reception early. Antonio followed her to an elegant brownstone nestled among the rich on Madison Avenue.

Before she could put her key in the front door Antonio approached her, clearing his throat loudly.

"Excuse me, Mrs. Hudson," he said and, with a slight bow, gave her the yellow envelope marked "Urgent." Then he drove off into the moonless city's darkness.

She opened the envelope, nearly dropped the photos, and then raced indoors to watch the video. Throwing the photos in every direction, she screamed and phoned her attorney. The next day's big, black headlines in The New York Times and Daily News blasted the news that Attorney General Glenn Hudson had resigned due to a serious health crisis.

A week later Hudson flew to Cabo San Lucas in Mexico and rented a cabin by the sea, his divorce papers crushed in his suitcase. The hotel maid, holding a crisp hundred-dollar bill in her hand, gladly gave Antonio the key to Hudson's room.

He entered silently. Hudson, naked, was on the bed drinking whiskey and masturbating while watching a porn flick.

"Enjoying yourself, motherfucker?" Antonio growled.

Hudson jumped out of bed, spilling his drink.

"Who the hell are you? How did you get in here?"

Antonio leaned casually against the bedroom door, stroking his Glock handgun affectionately.

"Remember Sheila Haines?"

Hudson's eyes bugged.

"You've treated her quite badly. You abandoned her. You left her with an underground abortionist who raped and nearly killed her. You discarded her like dirt," Antonio said calmly, but with narrowed eyes as hard as steel.

Hudson screamed, "Hey, we can work it out. It's a simple misunderstanding."

"Not so simple, asshole," Antonio bellowed. "Sheila sends her regards."

Hudson's body lay twisted on the carpet in a spreading pool of blood.

An hour later Antonio stretched out in his private jet back to Tuscany and snoozed.

***

Father Callahan turned around when he heard the brisk clip of high heels behind him on the sidewalk of the rectory. Sheila tugged lightly on his cassock sleeve, radiant.

"Ah, lassie, you look like a spring rose," the priest said with a smile.

"Thanks to you and Dr. Peters. I leave for Tuscany in two hours."

"A holiday?"

"More than that. My apartments are sold."

"Why Italy?"

"I'm beginning a new life and will be staying with my childhood friend Antonio at his villa in Tuscany."

A generous grin spread over his face, because he suspected that Antonio was far more than a childhood friend.

"By the way," he said, "I've learned from The New York Times that Glenn Hudson was murdered in Mexico."

"Ah yes," she said, "so have I."

They smiled companionably, as if enjoying a private joke.

Bernice had been watching them from the greenhouse doorway, a cloud of shock and darkness covering her face. The stunningly beautiful young woman had held Father Callahan's hand and kissed him on the cheek, and in parting they had hugged affectionately.

"Take care and be safe," she heard the priest say as he followed her to the limo. "God protect you, lassie."

Bernice watched him lift his arms protectively toward the woman, who waved a little teddy bear out the window.

"I will miss you," the woman said with eyes that were clearly moist.

Bernice, with a strong edge to her voice, asked a greenhouse volunteer, "Who is that woman?"

"Perhaps his sister," the man suggested.

He had kissed and hugged this woman. Why had he not hugged or kissed her?

CHAPTER 22

Snowflakes fluttered on Woofy's nose as she jumped, rolled, and chased her tail around and around the greenhouse. He enjoyed her playfulness in the light snow but had little love for the approach of winter. He still yearned for the lush moors of Ireland and for the serenity of the monastery, which now felt like a distant dream.

Once more he read Sheila's letter.

Dear Friend,

I love Italy, the home of my grandparents. I've been traveling in Europe with Antonio enjoying Rome, France and England. I have some good news. I am engaged to Antonio, getting married come May. I never thought I could be so happy. Come to Italy. Stay at our villa estate and please marry us.

With Love,

Sheila.

Enclosed were photos of her in the arms of a striking young man in front of his sprawling vineyard. Sheila was happy and safe, and it warmed his heart.

Getting married so soon? Why should he be surprised? Sheila was young, smart and gorgeous — and now in the land of hot Italian men.

Visit and marry them? What an exciting proposition, and perhaps a chance to visit his parents and sister in Dublin. Then the idea of visiting Irish monasteries saddened him when his thoughts flashed on Abbot Jules' cruel and unfounded accusations.

He remembered his dear friend, Brother Thaddeus, who
taught him how to chant the divine office, with a bass voice that
remained vibrant at ninety. His monastic life had been a happy, serene
experience of prayer and laughter, especially at evening meals. He
missed all of it, and it was a raw pain that continued to live in his
heart.

In New York, nothing was as it had been. Monastic silence
had been replaced with the endless noise of a huge city. Despite his
frustrations, as a confessor he was expected to listen passively to
people's revelations of their life's traumas and sins.

Father Alex hated him and had cursed him to Hell, and he
had not yet found a way to deal with his persistent attraction toward
Bernice.

A trip to Italy would do his heart good, yet May seemed eons in
the waiting, and he dared not think of what might become of him by
then. He would enjoy meeting Antonio; he had a strong suspicion that
it was Antonio who had sent Glenn Hudson to perdition.

All things considered, the past few days had been relatively calm
but he still felt edgy. Casey was keeping his nose to the grindstone but
still had made no breakthroughs in the serial killer's case. It was all
depressing.

"Don't let it get to you. Just a matter of time before the killer
will strike again. Then you can crucify him," Callahan had told his
friend.

"You really think so?" asked the downcast detective.

"Without a shadow of a doubt."

He put Woofy on a new blue leash and they left for their regular
Saturday romp in Central Park. She tugged like a Husky with her tail
lifted high, swinging in the air.

Father Alex stood at the top of the stairs, listening for
movements on the first floor. Rosemary would be shopping for at least
two more hours. Derrick was always gone on weekend afternoons,
somewhere. The greenhouse volunteers had finished their work for
the day. He prided himself on knowing the comings and goings of
everyone who assumed he was invisible.

He toddled to the rectory basement humming "All Praise to
the Lord" and opened a closet. He knelt to snatch a can of gasoline,

matches, old newspapers and rags from under the bottom shelf. With considerable effort, he gripped the doorknob and heaved himself up.

Then he shuffled to the greenhouse in his old, tattered plaid pajamas and dirty slippers. He glanced toward the city streets, fairly empty of walkers, cabs and buses typical of late Saturday afternoons on the West side … satisfied.

He opened the greenhouse door and began pouring gasoline on the shelves. He felt no reverence for these innocent flowers, basking in the warmth of sunlight. He threw the burning rags onto the shelves, euphoric when flames burst high in the air.

Rosemary returned early from shopping and dropped her bags of groceries on the rectory steps when she saw Alex scurry out of the greenhouse, holding a gasoline can. Behind him, waves of fire leaped high.

She ran to the kitchen, called 9-1-1, and held onto the kitchen counter, shaking. When Alex entered the rectory she shouted, "My God, you've lost your mind! I'll tell the firemen what you did!"

At that, he sprang to her face and doused her blouse with gasoline.

"No, you won't! I'll tell him you did it. They'll smell the gasoline on your clothes."

She froze. Alex fled to his room, opened his window, pounded his fists on the window ledge in excitement and shouted, "Burn to Hell."

Fire engines rolled in. The firemen rolled out hoses and fought the raging fire to keep it from spreading to the church and rectory. Rosemary tore off her blouse, put on a sweater and ran out of the rectory, frantic.

After the fire was contained the battalion chief approached her as she stood by the rectory fence, biting her nails. He took off his gloves, wiping thick ash from his sweaty face.

"Damn lucky the rectory and church still stand, just twenty feet from the greenhouse in the back. I'd tear down the remains if I were you."

"Some creep must have set this fire," he added, shaking his head.

"Lots of druggies and homeless people roam these parts," she replied. "Any one of them could have set the fire." She hated to deceive him but had no idea what she should do.

The arson investigator arrived, a short, thin man wearing glasses, looking more like a CPA. He scanned the backyard carefully, picking through the ashes, seething.

"Arson!" he shouted, making notes and taking pictures.

The firemen rolled up their hoses and were prepared to leave when Father Callahan arrived, flabbergasted. He picked up Woofy, who was trembling. Rosemary rushed to him.

"The arson investigator says someone set the fire," unable to look him in the eye. "It might have been worse had I not come back early from shopping," she said, blessing herself repeatedly.

"Where is Alex?"

"In his room," she mumbled.

The battalion chief approached them.

"We'll be back tomorrow. I need to make sure no fire pockets remain smoldering." He smiled at Rosemary. "You saved the rectory and church. Too bad about the greenhouse."

Callahan handed Woofy to Rosemary.

"Please put her in my bedroom with her toys and close the door." He walked through the ashes and the thick smoke, amazed that a few feet of the greenhouse remained.

His heart was heavy for the hundreds of tender flowers ruthlessly destroyed, and for the loss of all the good they could have offered the sick and homebound.

He heard a noise and looked up. Alex was closing his window and the window shades.

CHAPTER 23

Callahan approached Rosemary, who was sitting anxiously in the living room.

"We need to talk."

She sat up on the couch, fighting back tears.

"Please tell me, who really set the fire?"

She cast her eyes down, silent.

"You can trust me," he said, gentling his voice. "You have nothing to fear from me."

Rosemary lifted her head.

She raised her voice in anger. "Alex did it! He came into the rectory with a gasoline can, yapping like a hyena. I told him flat out I was going to report him to the fire chief. That's when he sprayed my blouse with gasoline, threatened to tell them I started the fire ... that roach."

Every muscle in his body tensed. So it had come to this, Alex's hatred, his revenge and his craziness.

"Come with me. We need the privacy of the church sacristy," and he took her trembling hand in his. He closed the sacristy door and chose his words with the greatest of care.

"Alex is dangerous and unpredictable. He must be removed from here before he kills us all. God only knows what he is capable of. I am phoning Bishop Graham now."

He took the bishop's card from his wallet and dialed. Rosemary took out her rosary beads, kissed the crucifix, and began praying. The phone rang for long minutes and, as Callahan was about to hang up, Bishop Graham finally answered.

"I'm sorry to bother you," he said, identifying himself. "We have a dangerous situation on our hands." Bishop Graham listened, and Callahan knew he was fuming.

"When did the fire start?"

"Two hours ago."

"Do you honestly believe Rosemary telling you that Father Alex set the fire?"

"On my life I do," he said with no hesitation.

"Are you on a private line?"

"Yes, Your Eminence."

"Remain where you are. I'll get back to you shortly."

They waited, numb, their nerves on end.

When the phone rang, Rosemary jumped in her chair. Drips of sweat ran down Callahan's neck.

"I'm sorry you've had to go through such a dreadful situation," Bishop Graham said without waiting for his response. "What I plan to do for Father Alex will be very disturbing. Please be prepared."

Callahan's head began to pound unmercifully.

"We'll arrive within the hour."

The phone clicked off before Callahan could ask what he was supposed to be prepared for, so they sat on the rectory steps stiff, silent and waiting. Rosemary kept wiping her eyes until her apron pocket filled with wet tissues. Eventually a white van and a sleek, black Buick sedan drove up and parked in front of the rectory.

Bishop Graham emerged from his car in the company of a dignified, white-haired man dressed in a gray suit. Two strong young men dressed in hospital whites leaped out of the van. Bishop Graham approached Father Callahan and Rosemary.

"I'd like you to meet Dr. Rosen. He is the treating psychiatrist at Beacon private sanatorium. The doctor shook hands without warmth. Rosemary hurried into the rectory's living room, a nervous wreck.

"My hospital attendants," Dr. Rosen said, pointing to the two men putting on their vinyl gloves.

"Where is Father Alex?"

"In his room," Callahan said, pointing to the second floor.

"Has he ventured out?"

"Not at all." Bishop Graham sprang up the stairs to his room, knocking hard.

"Father Alex, open your door. This is Bishop Graham. I want to speak to you."

No response. The bishop came down the stairs, grim-faced.

"I need a key to his bedroom." Rosemary handed the spare key to the bishop from a kitchen drawer and hurried back to the security of the living room.

Dr. Rosen and his attendants followed the bishop up the staircase. He unlocked the door but was unable to get in.

"Looks like he's wedged something big against it," Bishop Graham said and stood aside. "This isn't going to get any easier," he added under his breath.

The men pushed hard, and harder, and gradually the door budged open and dislodged the dresser that had been pushed against it. Bishop Graham entered the room alone. Dr. Rosen and his attendants stood by the doorway watching. No one uttered a word.

Coughing from the foul smell, Graham quickly put a handkerchief to his nose, breathing through his mouth. Dirty clothes, food and wine bottles cluttered the room. The toilet stunk like a sewer, and the bedroom was filthy beyond reasonable description.

"Father Alex," he said in a kindly tone. "You're in a terrible state. You need help urgently. I am sending you to a top-grade sanatorium. They will help get you back on your feet."

Alex crawled about on the floor screaming in a high, shrill, unnatural voice.

"I don't need your help!"

"You most certainly do."

He paused a moment, watching Alex dig his nails into the soiled carpet.

"We have an eyewitness who saw you burning down the greenhouse. God help us, the fire could have taken down this rectory and church. Please stand up and put on your bathrobe and come with me. Try to keep the last shreds of . . ." He stopped mid-sentence.

Alex was beyond responding to anything remotely sensible. He crumpled in a fetal position, back against the wall, and wet his pants.

"No! No! You can't force me to go anywhere."

Disheartened, Bishop Graham left the bedroom. The doctor's attendants restrained Alex, who fought and bit trying to free himself from their firm grip. Dr. Rosen quickly took a syringe from his medical bag and plunged it into Alex's arm. In seconds his body grew limp.

Sickened, Callahan watched the drama unfold. Alex was put into a straightjacket and carried out to the unmarked van, followed by Dr. Rosen.

"Terribly sad," Bishop Graham said to Callahan, washing his hands with soap up to his elbows. "Sanitize and strip the second floor to its bare bones, and get rid of every inch of furniture. Burn all of Alex's clothes. Everything in that foul room is a stinking disaster. Don't wait on it."

"It will be done immediately," Father Callahan assured him. "What's going to happen to Father Alex?" As much as he despised Alex's behavior, he was shocked at the extreme measures that had been taken.

"He'll have excellent medical care and for as long as it takes. I have retired priests who will gladly take turns staying with him until he's able to be alone. He will be suffering, confused and afraid when he wakes up. I'm on my way right now to be with him and offer him solace."

"I find that rather kind given what Father Alex has done," Callahan complained.

"Father, let us remember that kindness and compassion are our priestly calling, and who among us is without fault? Father Alex was not always in this despicable condition. He was once a brilliant and dynamic priest, but he has been destroyed by the bottle."

Father Callahan, chastised and embarrassed, said, "Please forgive me for my harsh judgment and unkind attitude."

"And for mine as well," Bishop Graham added. "When Father Alex is able to leave the hospital, I will send him to a home for retired priests to live out the rest of his days. Saint Michael's Retirement Center is a magnificent home. Priests from all over the country are on the waiting list to live there," he said with a smile.

"I am glad for him," Callahan said, sincerely, but unable to forget the sight of Father Alex's limp body.

"On Monday I'll send Father Backer to get the church's financial books in order. It won't take long. He used to handle the archdiocesan finances for decades, recently retired at eighty . . . well . . . kind of," he said with a grin.

Bishop Graham anticipated Callahan's answer but pressed on with a question.

"Would you like to take over as pastor?"

"No," Callahan said quickly.

"In that case, how about serving as the acting pastor for a brief stretch, until I can appoint a new pastor?"

"If that's just a short time, I suppose I can manage," Callahan said unhappily.

"That's a good thing," Bishop Graham said as he put on his coat. He had no intention of hurrying the process.

* * *

Callahan sat at the dining room table, sipping a cup of tea with Rosemary in a calmer mood.

"Bishop Graham said Father Alex would be getting the best of care."

"Of course," she said icily. "Monday we have to get commercial cleaners in here and clean the upstairs down to the floor nails." Then she perked up. "I expect life will get better now that Alex is gone."

"Let's hope so," he said, unable to shake the feeling that hope felt frail and uncertain.

CHAPTER 24

Early Monday morning, strips of sunlight squeezed between the city's tightly knit buildings. He treaded gingerly over piles of ash, wood and broken glass in the rectory's backyard where the thriving greenhouse had been.

In vain he tried to expunge his anger toward Alex, despite Bishop Graham's admonition to be forgiving. The greenhouse had been a sanctuary of laughter and delight where volunteers prepared baskets of beautiful flowers for the church and its homebound parishioners. All that had been destroyed by Alex's mad revenge.

He thought of Thron, and found himself longing for the little monk's wise counsel.

Two trucks of commercial cleaners arrived, and six men unloaded their tools and equipment. Soon they had ripped out the upstairs carpets and drapes and removed beds, dressers, and every other stick of furniture as well as the sinks, toilets and tubs. They scrubbed the floor to its bare nails and cleaned heavy dirt from all the windows. After seven hours of intense labor, every square inch had been cleaned and sanitized like a surgical room.

The foreman approached Callahan.

"Got to tell you, Father, the upstairs was real nasty for a rectory," he said, disgusted. "You'll get the bill this week."

Embarrassed, Callahan mumbled, "The man living upstairs was terribly sick, now in hospital," looking past him.

"Damn!" the foreman said. "Don't go upstairs for twenty-four hours. The place needs to dry out. Most of the floors are rotten. Need to replace them."

He drove off, hauling two Dumpsters filled to the brim, covered with tarps flapping in the wind.

As they left, the gardeners rolled in with another Dumpster. Depressed, he watched them remove wood and glass from the burned greenhouse, then hose down the yard from one end to the other, a sorry mix of dirt and ash.

After they left, he walked toward the rectory, emotionally spent. Bernice had been gone for a week's holiday, but soon she arrived in a jovial spirit, parking her Jaguar in the rectory's driveway.

She opened the rectory backyard gate and fell on her knees, screaming, "My God, what's happened?"

He rushed to her and steadied her back on her feet, brushing off ash and dirt from her wool coat.

"Come into the rectory. I'll explain." He led her into the living room.

She sat on the couch in tears.

"My greenhouse. My beautiful flowers destroyed," twisting her hands back and forth.

"Someone set the greenhouse on fire. We don't know who," he said. "Thanks to Rosemary, the firemen saved the church and rectory from destruction."

"Didn't Father Alex see the fire?" she asked. "He's always in his room."

"He's been too sick to notice anything, and was taken to hospital after the fire."

She searched his eyes tearfully. He held his breath, shading the truth.

"How awful," she finally said.

"How about a cup of tea?" he said, ignoring the tense knots in his back."

"That will help," she said. They sat in the dining room quietly, until Bernice looked up toward the second floor stairs, sniffing the disinfectant.

"What happened upstairs?"

"It's been in bad shape for years. After Father Alex went to the hospital I had the second floor cleaned from top to bottom," unwilling to give her more details. His tea tasted bitter, and he wanted Bernice gone.

She sipped her tea slowly and thoughtfully.

"Listen," she said softly. "I can get the greenhouse restored to its former grandeur in no time. I'd like to renovate the second floor too, get all the walls painted, put in new drapes, floors and furnishings. It will look just fabulous with new bedrooms and bathrooms," she said, a sweet smile of optimism brightening her face.

"You've done too much already," he said wearily, wanting to be left alone.

"How about if I start in a week?" she asked.

"How thoughtful of you," he said.

"I'd like to go upstairs now and see what needs doing?"

"Sorry, but it's still too wet. Holding off a couple of days will be better," he said.

"No problem."

She flew excitedly to his side and kissed him fleetingly from cheek to cheek, depositing a sponge of red on his face, and drove off.

He shut the rectory's front door. The softness of her kiss lingered. Damn. Just as he spread out his long legs to rest in the living room couch, the doorbell rang. He ignored it until he couldn't stand the noise. Casey smiled when he finally opened the door, but the priest didn't try.

"Jeez, what's been going on around here?"

"We had a fire, and the greenhouse was destroyed."

"So I noticed. Know who done it?" Callahan took his time arranging lies in tidy order. "The arson investigator said someone set the fire, no doubt a drunk or homeless person."

Casey grinned wickedly. "I bet that ghastly drunk upstairs is the drunk who torched the place. Jeez, it smells like a morgue upstairs."

"What makes you think that Alex did it?" He was shocked that Casey had nailed it immediately.

"Come on, Padre, I'm not some fossil. I see a lot, feel a lot, know a lot, been here a whole lot. So where has he been stashed?"

"In a hospital," and left it at that. "Bernice offered to rebuild the greenhouse and to renovate the rectory's second floor," he said stiffly.

Casey smirked.

"Of course she did."

"Today is not a good time for whatever you want," Callahan said, showing him the door.

"Sorry about that," Casey said, but he ignored the priest's annoyance and pushed himself inside.

"I've been thinking about The Dragon pawnshop. It's just a feeling, but there might be a faint possibility the assassin returned. How about if we go back to the pawnshop and see if he's came back with something?"

"Go yourself."

"Come on, Padre, I don't have your tender touch, speaking Mandarin, bowing and the like. Tell you what. We can get some Chinese. It's on me, and it won't take long."

Still no answer.

"Hey, from what I see around here, a change of scenery and smell will do you good. By the way, I have a comfy Chrysler sedan, a rental, because my truck's in the shop."

In spite of himself, Callahan laughed.

"Okay, but let's pass on the food. I have no appetite."

"Fine with me."

* * *

They walked toward the back room of the restaurant, which was again packed from wall to wall with people. Security recognized them and pushed open the heavy drape. It felt as if they had never left.

The pawnshop owner stood behind his counter and smiled at Callahan. Security inched forward. He placed his spotless dragon statue on the counter in front of the pawnshop owner, bowing slightly.

"This dragon is so beautiful," he said in Mandarin. "Perhaps you did not notice the emeralds. They appear real and very expensive."

Casey shifted from foot to foot, impatient to get to the serious matter at hand.

"No mistake," the old man said, with a slip of a smile. "I know well this dragon. Keep it."

"I am grateful," he said and put it back in its velvet pouch and into his jacket.

"My friend," Callahan said gesturing toward Casey, "wondered if the man who brought in the ring and gun returned?"

"Often do," the pawn store owner said, "here yesterday."

Casey's eyebrows lifted like little arrows. "Did he look the same?"

"Yes."

"What did he bring in?"

"A gun . . . will sell."

Casey turned to Father Callahan.

"It's worth buying. Might still have fingerprints." He put on his latex gloves, examining it carefully.

"Did you touch it?"

"Handle."

Casey inspected it closer. "Man, oh man, this is a Tabuk marksman rifle used in the Russian army, made in Iraq."

"Would ordinary cops know about such a gun?" Callahan asked, admiring Casey's knowledge.

"Only gun nuts like me. Rifles and guns fascinated me as a teen. When it comes to guns, I'm a full-bore encyclopedia."

"I didn't see any guns in your house."

"I don't have any, except my service revolver."

"A contradiction, given your fascination?" Casey grinned.

"Well, Padre, of all people you should know life is a trash can of contradictions."

He forked over two hundred dollars to the old man, to be billed later to the police department.

After dropping off Callahan at the rectory, he took the rifle to the police lab, praying to God for a break.

The lab tech, a bone-skinny, middle-aged man, looked oddly at Casey and wondered why a retired detective was asking for a favor. Still, he studied the rifle carefully under his scope then handed it, tagged and wrapped in plastic, back to Casey. "It has two different sets of fingerprints, one on the stock and the other inside the chamber. Looks like someone did a sloppy job cleaning the prints off."

The lab tech took note of Casey's disappointment. "Keep the faith," he said, and returned to a pile of work.

"Keep the faith" did nothing but piss Casey off. With despair overwhelming his hope, he turned over the fingerprints to Chief Duffy, who gave them to the FBI.

* * *

In just a few weeks, Bernice's crew of carpenters, tradesmen and interior designers had the rectory's second floor completely renovated.

"Come up here," she called to Callahan. "I want to show you the new second floor."

He bounded up the stairs, eager to see the results.

The fact that Bernice would be out of the rectory was a relief. He had spent most of his time hiding in the church basement, taking Woofy for long walks, or working in the rectory office with his door closed.

The last of the workmen had left, and everything smelled new and fresh. "What do you think?" she asked, clearly thrilled with the results.

He liked the walls, painted in almond, and the cream-colored drapes in the two bedrooms. The queen-size beds were covered with light green bedspreads. Each room had pine furniture on light brown carpets. He ran his hands over the new porcelain bathtubs.

"You've outdone yourself," he said. "My God, the expense for all of this must be outrageous."

"It's of no consequence," she said.

"I can never thank you enough."

She giggled.

"I'm delighted you like it." She had naughty ideas of how he could thank her, and giggled again.

Even the outside of the rectory's brownstone had been sanded, with sparkling new windows. The greenhouse looked as if it had never been burned to the ground. The volunteers were back, tending to the flowers.

Bernice's generosity seemed endless. Although he was grateful, the unsettling question remained: Why? Why was she so generous?

Derrick enjoyed teasing Callahan whenever he could get away with it. As he was leaving the rectory with an open bag of popcorn in his hands, the custodian snickered, "Holy man of god, Bernice has the hots for you."

"Good thing you're fast on your feet, laddie," the irritated priest grumbled.

* * *

After hearing the confessions of the elementary school children — again a session of wriggly, gun-chewing, stinky kids who recited memorized sins from their catechism books — he returned to the rectory.

Being the acting pastor wasn't too bad, all things considered. Still, he worried if Bishop Graham had purposefully forgotten to appoint a new pastor. He thought about Ireland, and then about the Zen monastery. *Where is peace? Will joy elude me? Am I lost in sin for all the days of my life?*

CHAPTER 25

The memory of Alex's limp body, tied in a straitjacket and hauled off to Beacon Sanatorium, haunted him. What kind of shape Alex might be in was a wrenching question. The fact they had hated each other, that they had damned each other to hell, made it worse. Unable to stand the pressure any longer, he called Bishop Graham.

"I've been concerned about Father Alex. How is he coming along?"

"You need not worry," the bishop said cheerfully. Father Alex is out of the hospital and in residence at Saint Michael's Retirement Center in Monroe, New York. How about paying him a surprise visit?"

Before he could also ask when the new pastor would be arriving, Bishop Graham said, "God bless you," and the phone clicked off.

Visit Alex? Would the old priest refuse to see him, given their mutual animosity? He paced the floor in the rectory's living room and decided, come what may, he would risk visiting Alex. He left Woofy in the care of Rosemary. The dog now had the complete run of the rectory, but she would not explore the second floor even though the menacing Alex was no longer there.

He drove to Monroe, rolling down his car windows, filling his lungs with crisp air after a light snow. He yearned for spring to hurry up and to sprout tender leaves after winter's long snooze. The air lifted his spirit through a haze of anxiety. Would Alex refuse to see him? Throw a fit?

He drove to a gas station, and a young man filled up his gas tank, washed his windows, checked his oil, water and tires, and cleaned his windshield.

"Happen to know where Saint Michael's Retirement Center is?"

"Sure. Go five miles ahead, turn right at the fork in the road, and go up the hill to the center. Can't miss it."

He drove a mile but then turned off to a side road and stopped.

Go back. You don't need to see Alex. He was a sorry excuse for a priest, and he began to drive back to the city.

Two miles later he pulled off the road and stopped again, massaging his throbbing temples.

Coward! Have you forgotten your own dark, sinful past? Admit the truth. Not much has changed in your heart and mind, yet you condemn Father Alex.

He made another U-turn and drove resolutely back to the retirement center, where stately evergreens lined the sides of the road leading to a large stone building. He parked in front, hesitating yet again, then moved slowly up the center's stairs and rang the doorbell, listening to its musical chimes. He felt hot despite the biting cold wind.

Father Alex himself opened the door. Callahan pulled back, transfixed by the new man, clean-shaven, twenty pounds heavier, his hair grown back thick, curly and white, a rather attractive elderly man. If it weren't for a small pink birthmark near the hairline on the left side of Alex's forehead, Callahan would not have believed he was the same man.

"At last you've come."

Alex took his hand and shook it warmly. "Please come in. Our center is as beautiful as you are," he said joyfully.

Speechless, Callahan followed him to a large empty sitting room filled with soft ivory couches and dainty statues of saints in each corner.

"I barely recognized you," Callahan said.

"I hardly recognize myself," Father Alex replied, laughing full throttle. "I am no longer a sack of bones and gristle. I don't even need glasses. How do you like my long mane?" And he wove his fingers playfully through his hair.

Caught up with his gaiety, Callahan said, "I love it — and you've gained thirty years of youth." The older man's face flushed with happiness. Callahan had never seen him happy, nor ever heard him laugh.

Father Alex folded his hands in a prayerful steeple.

"I regret from the depths of my heart how I lived, and how I treated you and more people than I can count. I chose to lose my footing after a long career. I ask for your mercy and forgiveness," Alex said, gazing at him like a prodigal son returning to his father.

"It is I who is in need of your forgiveness," Callahan said contritely, with the painful knowledge that his own life of sin and hatred was beyond description.

"Forgiveness, a precious gift from Christ bestowed upon us unworthy sinners," Father Alex said, kissing Callahan's hand.

Confounded by his loving act of humility, the younger man had no idea of how to respond.

"Come with me. You are in time for lunch."

His voice grew strong and exuberant. Elderly priests sat companionably with each other enjoying conversation and their lunch from long buffet tables filled with salads, chicken, soups, fruit and dessert.

"Do you miss being the pastor at Saint Francis of Assisi?"

"No. I was pastor in name only, and for too many years," Alex said as he chewed on a chicken bone.

When they had finished lunch, Father Alex rose.

"Today I am the greeter at the center. Visitors come here at all hours. I enjoy supervising the little children in our playroom. I love my life here," he said, his eyes glowing.

"I am happy for you," said Callahan, holding his emotions tight.

"Did you know that Bishop Graham visits me every Saturday? He spends afternoons with me. Such a precious friend."

That definitely took Callahan by surprise. He could only guess how busy the bishop was. About to ask if Alex had any family visitors, he thought better of it.

"Father Abrams will show you around. I must attend to my duties."

"That won't be necessary. I must get back to the parish."

"Did you know also that Bishop Graham is becoming the archbishop in San Francisco? He is delighted with his appointment. He told me he has family in the Bay Area."

"No. I had no idea."

"He also promised to visit me twice a month, rather amazing considering the distance." A smile illumined his face.

That Bishop Graham would go out of his way to such an extreme was baffling. "I'll visit you as well," he offered spontaneously.

"No need, really."

"But I want to."

Father Alex studied him wistfully.

"I would enjoy your visit, but now I must get going. See you soon." He left with a bounce in his step.

Callahan waved good-bye to this new man of God, no longer lost. When he returned to the parish, he saw that Rosemary had left the Diocesan newspaper on the dining table. On the front page was a striking photo of Bishop Graham announcing his elevation to archbishop in the San Francisco archdiocese, an astonishing accomplishment at just 35 years old.

After six that evening the rectory doorbell rang. At the front door stood Bishop Graham. "I thought I'd stop by on my way to Saint Michael's Retirement Center.

"Please come in."

"I was up there earlier. I can't believe the transformation in Father Alex."

"I know. He was delighted with your visit. Something smells mighty good."

"Please join me. We have hot stew on the stove, and fresh cornbread on the table."

"Wonderful," he said, swinging his coat over a chair in the dining room. "I haven't had a morsel since breakfast.

"Delicious," he said, into his second bowl of stew, and wiping cornbread crumbs from his lips. He pushed back his chair. "A fine dinner indeed. I didn't realize how famished I was."

"Every time I've been with Father Alex he's asked about you, and has been heartsick in the way he treated you."

"I have only myself to blame. I intend to visit him at least twice a month, maybe more."

"I'm sure he would have appreciated that."

"Would have? I don't understand."

"Shortly after you left he felt tired, according to Father Abrams, and went early to his room to take a nap. He died peacefully reading his prayer book with the page turned to the Twenty-Third Psalm, 'The Lord Is My Shepherd.'"

"My God. I regret not having seen him sooner."

"Life is filled with regrets. They will eat us alive unless we release them. I will be officiating at his funeral at noon tomorrow."

"Any family?"

"Only me; he was my father."

"I need to remember that we are all Fathers in Christ."

"No, Father Callahan. I'll tell you this in confidence. Father Alex was my father, by blood. I found this out just a few weeks ago."

"I don't understand," said Callahan, flabbergasted.

"When I was a few months old, I was placed at St. Mary's, a Catholic orphanage, and the Graham family adopted me. Eventually they told me that my mother had died a few months after my birth and I was given up for adoption. The fact is, I was never curious about my birth parents until recently."

Father Callahan listened, stone still.

"I found it strange that I should be curious now, but I went to Saint Mary's office. The orphanage was torn down years ago, but I pressured the Mother Superior to give me my adoption files to read.

"I sat in her office wearing my bishop's garb, aware I would be in for a battle. 'What can I do for you, Your Eminence?' she asked. 'My adoptive parents' names are George and Heather Graham,' I told her. 'I want to read my adoption papers.'

"She glared at me hard. 'You know that all adoption papers are confidential, Your Excellency, and not available for anyone.'

"I rose from my chair. 'I insist on seeing my records!' and I admit that I bellowed like a bull. 'Very well.' She left in a huff, slamming the door behind her. It took thirty minutes before she returned and gave me the file.

"'Against my better judgment, I shall permit you to read the file, but you cannot make copies, nor take them with you.'"

"Nuns are real tough," Father Callahan smiled.

Bishop Graham laughed, "You'd better believe it."

"My mother's name was Ursula Acker. She lived in New York as an eighteen-year-old girl, and she had a brief affair, resulting in my birth. I wrote down my father's name, Max Heilberg, and his birthdate, assuming he lived somewhere in New York State. I hired a private investigator to find him.

"When I did, I was shocked senseless to find out that Max Heilberg's middle name was Alex and, of all things, he had become a priest, and in my own diocese no less."

"My God! Did you tell him?"

"Are you serious? Of course not," his eyes darkened. "I only wanted to love him, and to care for him. My heart is heavy because I no longer can do that," and his voice broke.

"I am sorry he is no longer in your life. Thank you for revealing such a delicate matter to me."

Graham nodded, drawing in a ragged breath.

"I needed to. I wanted you to know about his peaceful death."

"I enjoyed the dinner," he added. Then he put on his coat, sighed heavily, and drove off to Saint Michael's Retirement Center.

Callahan sat for hours in the living room, in shock. In his heart he felt Father Alex had waited for their visit and died thereafter, embraced with the love of God. Bishop Graham's personal revelations moved him deeply, as did the thought of his last visit with Father Alex. He wept.

* * *

Early next morning he returned to Saint Michael's in time for Father Alex's funeral Mass. The sun rested high in the sky; it eased its light through the large, oval, stained-glass windows and warmed the cherry casket. Tall candles burned on gold candelabras, their flames rising as if in prayer.

Bishop Graham, in white vestments, said his father's memorial Mass, chanting, "Lord have mercy, Christ have mercy." He left the sanctuary swinging a gold censer of frankincense over his father's casket.

Out of the blue he handed his censer to the priest standing beside him, then bent low before the casket, spreading his arms and hands over it and kissing the cross. In a loud voice, he intoned, "God bless you, my dearest Father," paused, then said, "In the name of Christ."

The casket was moved toward the entry of the chapel. Bishop Graham prayed solemnly, *"The Lord is my shepherd. I shall not want. He makes me to lie down in green pastures. He leads me beside the still waters. He restores my soul. He leads me in the paths of righteousness for His name's sake. Yea, though I walk through the valley of the shadow of death, I will fear no evil, for you are with me. Your rod and your staff, they comfort me. You prepare a table before me in the presence of my enemies. You anoint my head with oil. My cup runs over. Surely goodness and mercy shall follow me all the days of my life, and I will dwell in the house of the Lord forever."*

CHAPTER 26

His last visit with Father Alex continued to live in his heart and mind, filling him with a profound sense of unworthiness. He subscribed to the San Francisco diocesan newsletter to keep up with Bishop Graham's administrative progress. In a short time he had brought the archdiocese from the brink and into solvency.

Friday evenings he and Derrick enjoyed poker and other card games, fortified with root beer floats and heaping bowls of caramelized popcorn.

Looking forward to a relaxing evening with Derrick, he was strolling toward his room in the church basement when a heavy whiff of weed hit him.

Derrick, unaware of the priest's presence, sat on the edge of his bed, squeezing his hands on his head, lost in another world. By the look on his face, it was a world no one else dared enter.

He tapped lightly on his door. Derrick jumped to his feet, snuffing out his joint on the ashtray by his nightstand, red-faced. Callahan pulled up a chair and sat next to him.

"Sorry about the weed," Derrick said hoarsely, unable to look the priest in the eye.

"Worse things," he said. "Care to share what's troubling you?" He coughed from the smoke and opened the window.

Derrick rubbed his bloodshot eyes. "Fucking memories."

"I'm not here to be your judge or jury. I have my own demons to deal with."

Derrick leaned hard against the headboard of his bed. "Might help," he mumbled.

"Often does," Father Callahan urged.

He reached for another joint.

"Always Vietnam shit," he said, wiping driblets of sweat from his forehead. "Colonel Becker, my commanding officer, took a real liking to me, made me his assistant doing odd jobs. Come late nights we'd play poker. I was just an innocent eighteen-year-old kid— impressed like hell that he liked me, and that he kept me out of the killing fields."

He slid off his bed, stood up and leaned against the wall, sucking in air.

"Three weeks had passed; we had finished a game of poker. Then he gave me a stiff shot of Scotch. I drank beer on rare occasions, but booze made me sick. Man, in seconds I was wasted, and I started to weave back to my tent. Becker pulled me back, ripped off my pants . . . begun sucking my dick. I was shocked. In my drunken state I didn't resist."

Derrick eyed Callahan, sweating from embarrassment. The priest listened with no hint of shock forthcoming.

"Becker fucked me, for how long we were at it I had no idea. Next morning when I woke up I was butt naked in a tent next to him. I had no idea how the hell I got there."

"You have no reason to condemn yourself, given those circumstances," Father Callahan offered calmly.

Derrick squinted, rubbing his eyes.

"Hell, Colonel Becker was married, had four-year-old twin girls. It was the shits. A couple of days later he gave me another drink. I refused, told him it made me sick. Didn't matter, he forced me to drink.

"My head began swimming. He stripped off my clothes. I was too terrified to move. He bent me over his desk and raped me."

"My God," Father Callahan said, putting his hands to his mouth. "How long did that go on?"

"Almost every day for three months. Becker threatened to send me into the killing fields if I didn't cooperate. God help me, I did. I was at his mercy."

The priest listened, controlling his sense of shock and revulsion.

"My wretched life changed in March of '75. I woke up at two in the morning with plans on how to kill the fuck. Day and night that's all I obsessed on. I think it kept me sane.

"Early morning in April '75, I hid a handgun in my boot, prepared to kill Becker the next time he took me out to the bush to rape me. He had me in his tent, ready to haul me to the bush, when his phone rang. I clearly heard someone yelling orders to line up his troops and to evacuate his unit right now. The Vietcong had taken control of Saigon.

"Hell, that crazed son of a bitch forced me onto the floor anyway and begun raping me like a maniac. I couldn't get my hand on my gun."

"Diabolical . . . insane," Callahan muttered through clenching teeth.

"The helos were landing, buzzing like locusts. The captain in the first helo jumped out —flabbergasted — no men waiting on the field to be airlifted out. He ran to Becker's tent, saw him fucking me on the floor and heard me screaming, 'Stop!'

"He took his forty-five and slammed it into Becker's temple, handcuffed the motherfucker, hauled his ass off to the helo, and took command of my unit. In thirty minutes we were starting our trip back to the USA.

"That situation saved you from killing Becker."

Derrick looked away.

"Becker was court-martialed and returned to his family in Wyoming. Every second of every day I still lived to punish the fuck."

"You got over it?"

"Sure. You want to know how?"

"Tell me."

"You'll hate me."

"Don't count on it."

"After my discharge I flew to Jackson Hole, Wyoming, near the small ranch where Becker lived with his family. I rented a beat-up truck, stayed at a cheap motel, paid cash for everything, and spent a week tracking his movements.

"He worked at an auto shop in town. I had grown a beard, dyed my hair jet black, dressed in old jeans, baseball hat, cowboy boots, blended in with the locals as best I could, pretending to look for work."

"You did all that?"

"Needed to. I didn't want Becker recognizing me. One Friday night I went to the local joint across the street from where Becker worked and hung out. I hid way in the back, eating corn chips and drinking sodas. He finally came in the dive around eight . . . alone.

"Man, the joint was jumping. Lots of prostitutes busy working the place, skirts to their navels, tops open, boobs swinging every which way. Locals and tourists poured in there with wads of cash in their hands, wedding rings hidden . . . like dogs in heat.

"A pretty young girl waltzed up to Becker; both began drinking together while he pushed his fingers up her legs. He took her to a fleabag motel half a block down the road. I followed at a casual distance. The girl entered the hotel room first, with Becker looking around. I hung around waiting until he opened the door to leave. That's when the girl started yelling, 'I want my money.'

"He slammed his fist across her face, laughing. 'Not going to happen, bitch,' taking his time on the way back to his car. I followed him like a cat, my hand on my gun. He had parked a distance behind the hotel near a thick row of bushes. I crept up behind him and dug my gun into the base of his neck.

"'Get on your knees!' I yelled, and he did. 'Take my wallet,' he said.

"Don't want your fucking money. Put your hands behind your back.' I cuffed him, then turned him to face me. 'Remember me, asshole?' His eyes bugged out. 'Remember how you beat me, how you fucked me senseless, how you threatened to put me in the killing fields?'

"'You can't do this,' he whimpered — a sniffling coward.

"'You have a beautiful wife, young kids, and you're here screwing a prostitute.'" He went mute.

'I can kill you right here, or take you out of town and do it.'

'I have a family.'

'Oh yeah! Like you fucking care.'

"Becker started talking real fast. 'I'll change my ways.' I was so nervous I got light-headed, unaware I had lowered my gun to my side. That's all it took for Becker to lunge at me — and the gun went off.

"Damn. I thought I got shot." Derrick gulped a swig of water.

"Becker fell over on the ground. I stood there frozen. He didn't move. I took off the handcuffs and ran to my truck. I drove all night into Montana, then took a plane back to New York City.

"They never traced the gun to you?"

"Nope. I wore gloves, and the gun was stolen."

"Did he die?"

"Nope. But when he grabbed my gun he shot himself."

"Strange he never ratted you out."

"What good would it have done, given his military record, and nasty reputation in town?"

"What became of Becker?"

"His wife found out about his life with prostitutes, divorced him and remarried. The shot pierced his spine. He became a paraplegic, committed suicide a year later.

"You kept tabs on him?"

"Only enough to see what happened to him, but those memories still live in my head."

Father Callahan went to his side.

"It's time to focus on what's good in your life, Derrick. Talking to me about your trauma can free you of Becker. If not, my friend, he gets the last laugh."

"The last laugh?"

"For as long as you hate him, he's still controlling you," Callahan said, and he paused for a moment to collect his thoughts.

"I'm not all that you think I am," Callahan began slowly. "I have been hate personified. I've been revenge. I ran the streets in Belfast with killer thugs, the scum of the earth. I became the worst of the worst."

"That's hard to believe," Derrick said, mystified.

"I used women and discarded them like tissue paper. I had no conscience. I drank like a fish. I had no regard for myself or for anyone else in those horrid days. Thankfully, I met my wife and became a new man."

He rose and gently rested his hand on Derrick's shoulder. "My friend, it's but a faint whimper compared to what you went through in Vietnam."

Derrick rose from the edge of his bed. And for the first time in years he felt his heart and mind shed a heavy weight as he buried his face in Callahan's chest.

CHAPTER 27

At 8.a.m. Casey pounded on the rectory door. Callahan greeted him, taken aback by the detective's wild excitement and uncharacteristic cheerfulness. Casey hurried to the kitchen and poured himself a large cup of coffee, adding almost half a cup of cream. Clearly, he considered the rectory his second home.

"We've got a freaking break," Casey shouted as he snatched a glazed donut from the kitchen counter, pushed aside the New York Times and sat at the dining table.

"I'm all ears," Callahan said.

"Doug Smith is the police chief in Islip, out on Long Island. His daughter Heather lives on Elm Street in the Bronx, in a first-floor apartment near Fordham University. It's a quiet, working-class neighborhood. Yesterday she decided to go to Lake George with her boyfriend and stay a couple of days. She invited her girlfriend Arleen from Long Island to use her apartment so Arleen could see 'Evita' on Broadway."

Casey took a loud slurp of his coffee, then added a heaping tablespoon of sugar.

"Around three this morning, Arleen has the blanket ripped off her bed and she's terrified to see a guy standing over her. But she lets her Chihuahua sleep under her covers with her, and he goes apeshit, bites both the bastard's hands like a barracuda, rips up his gloves, draws blood, even bites his legs.

"And I gotta tell you, turns out Arleen is built like a rock, five-ten, a kick boxer, and she tears off the man's mask and kicks the shit out of him. He barely got away with his skin," Casey howled. "He must have been shocked shitless, 'cause he was expecting Chief Smith's daughter and Heather is short, and real petite."

"Thank God Heather was gone. That rat's luck is running out." Callahan said.

Casey nodded, feeling giddy.

"Now we have blood samples, bits of gloves and his mask. It was so dark that Heather could give only a partial description, but it's good enough. Said he has brown hair, around six feet tall, average build, scar under his chin. The tiny dog is named Chops, and now you know why. He took that fuck by surprise, that's for damned sure."

"How's the girl doing? And the dog?" Callahan asked.

"Arleen's fine. Already at the gym working out. Chops seemed upset until she rewarded him with a bowl of leftover steak."

"Maybe the department should trade in its German shepherd K-9s for some good Chihuahuas," Callahan said with a snicker.

"Those tiny critters are damned fearless," Casey said.

"Even with just a general description, it seems like this is the same guy who showed up in The Dragon pawnshop," Callahan said.

"Yeah. In an hour the lab will send us the DNA results. And next I'll be reviewing criminals' mug shots."

Callahan rocked back and forth in his straight chair. "Don't waste your time going through the criminals, Casey."

"What are you talking about?"

"I think you should investigate Chief Duffy's vice squad officers for starters."

Casey's mood blackened to something closer to normal as he pounded his fists on the table.

"Have you lost it, Padre?"

Callahan forced himself to keep calm.

"Think about how impeccably all these murders have gone down. Think about Chief Duffy's paranoia about corrupt police officers leaking in every crack of his police department. Think about those cop guns ending up in The Dragon's pawnshop. Think about how that creep gets through his victims' top security systems like he's brushing his teeth. In my book, that all adds up to an angry, sociopathic cop."

Casey began to sputter a protest in defense of his friends in blue, but then he froze stone still. Speechless in mid-sentence.

"I had a friend," Callahan said, lowering his voice as if a stranger had entered the room to listen. "He lived in Belfast in the time of The Troubles — a tough kid, a street fighter for the IRA."

"Were you close?"

"Mostly. Grew up in the same block. Brent carried a gun day and night for protection. It was dusk this one night when he headed home and heard a girl screaming in a back alley. He ran toward them and saw a British cop raping her."

"Damn!" Casey mumbled, and his eyes hardened to steel.

"He yelled at the top of his lungs . . . Stop! The cop pulled his sidearm and aimed it at Brent, but Brent was faster and shot the Brit point-blank in the head."

"The fuck had it coming," Casey said.

Callahan nodded.

"He peeled the cop off the girl and carried her home. The Brits combed the area like ravaging wolves looking for him, swearing they had a so-called eyewitness."

"What happened to Brent?"

"The IRA protected him and got him out of Belfast," Callahan said through an old anger that was thick in his throat. Casey's mind flashed to the dragon on Callahan's back. He was convinced that the priest was talking in code about himself.

"And your point is?"

"Sometimes cops are really bad men. I just feel this homicidal killer is in Chief Duffy's vice squad," Callahan said simply.

"Why haven't you mentioned these suspicions for all these weeks?"

"I didn't always think this way, but look at it from my point of view. You came to me to unload the burden of your investigation. You're a veteran police detective. I am just a priest, and confessor. Even a few weeks ago, I bet you would have laughed me into the graveyard."

"And why are you telling me this now?"

"Because now you will pay attention to what I have to say. Now you have fingerprints, and blood evidence. I know you don't want to believe bad things about other cops, but don't waste your time chasing river rats in gutters when this killer is much closer than that."

"You're suggesting that we investigate all the officers in Chief Duffy's vice squad?"

"Believe me, Casey, this is not a suggestion," the priest said icily. "Compare the DNA and fingerprints."

The thought of a cop assassin in the vice unit hit Casey like a major earthquake. Thirty minutes later he met with Chief Duffy in his home.

"How did you come up with this notion of a cop killer in Vice?" the skeptical chief asked.

"You've been telling me about dirty cops from day one, making me work like I'm in a freaking tomb. So, with no one else to bounce my ideas off, I talk to this Father Callahan in confession."

"There is nothing like the holy seal of confession," said Duffy, a devout Catholic. "You mentioned that this priest had a life before the priesthood?"

"Big time life. Grew up in Belfast, ran the streets in the days of The Troubles, educated in Oxford, high school principal, married, widower, then a monk in Ireland. He's street smart and he's no fucking wimp."

"That's enough for me. I'll pull all the vice squad officer files and match the information we get from the lab, fingerprints, blood, photos, all of it, and see who doesn't show up for work tomorrow. Anybody with those injuries to his hands and face is going to need to lay low for a while. And we should call all the ERs in the city." The chief smiled, broadly, for the first time in months.

That evening Casey phoned his cousin in Belfast. "Hey, you never got back to me. Know anything worth telling?"

"I didn't bother because of so many rumors. Lots of killings, lots of wild kids on the streets years past — and still."

"Of course," Casey said, pissed off, and hung up.

He walked his bedroom floor, unable to sleep. He couldn't shake the thought of Father Callahan's rage when he spoke about dirty cops. Now he and Chief Duffy had the mind-blowing task of hiding their secret investigation of the vice squad cops from Internal Affairs and the FBI. They would have to move fast.

At four in the morning, he collapsed on his bed in a depressed heap of stress and worry.

CHAPTER 28

Early Friday morning Chief Duffy arrived at Don's Café on the West
Side, empty except for a weary cook and waiter. Casey sat at a side
table munching on pancakes, well into his second cup of steaming
coffee.

As Duffy approached, his face was dark and tight. He carried a
large yellow file folder under his armpit.

"We finally have a solid ID, with fingerprints and blood evidence
of the serial killer." The chief's voice was barely audible.

"How bad is it?"

"Fucked to the wall."

There was a sickening pause. Casey leaned forward.

"It's that asshole Richard Madison, a vice cop in my division.
Been there five years, and in the department for ten. Gotta hand it to
you, Casey, directing me to vice."

"Nope, the credit goes to Father Callahan."

"Damned lucky," Duffy said, blessing himself twice with the
sign of the cross.

"What's your plan to nail Madison?"

"Here's the deal," Duffy said. "He has a second-floor apartment
in a warehouse in the seedy side of the Bronx. I want more evidence to
really seal his tomb, and it might be in that hole he lives in."

"Of course," Casey said. He drained his glass of ice water and
crunched the cubes between his teeth.

"The fuck took a few days off — claimed vacation time — more
like caring for his injuries from . . . what do you call that dog?"

"Chops the Chihuahua," Casey said, grinning. "And from that
tough-ass woman."

"I wonder if she'd like to join the force," Duffy said softly.

"Doubt it — more like the Army Rangers," Casey said with a
laugh.

Duffy cut him off.

"I want you to search Madison's apartment — right now. I have a couple of trusted retired cops following him. Right now he's at a doctor's office and I'm told they have a long line of patients waiting."

"Do I get backup?"

"No. I can't assign any active-duty cops to this until I know which ones I can trust. Pack your gun, get in and get out — fast. Remember, he is a vice cop, and they can smell trouble."

Duffy rose, kicked his chair and left.

Casey sped to the rectory, steaming. Madison, a vice cop he had helped train at the Police Academy in years past, just blowing his mind. Callahan was sitting on the rectory steps, petting Woofy.

"Happy day?"

"Worse than bad," Casey growled. "You were damn right. The serial killer is Richard Madison, a cop in Duffy's vice division. I even helped train the fuck in the academy. Duffy wants me to check out his apartment now and see if I can find more evidence to fully roast Madison's ass. Wanna come along? I could use a second set of eyes."

Callahan jumped into the front seat of Casey's truck, yelping.

"My God! You said you were going to replace these rocks."

"Someday. Fret not, Padre, at least you won't be dozing off."

He sped to Madison's address in the Bronx, on a seemingly vacant street filled with weary-looking warehouses. Inside, the building was dark as night. Casey pulled out his flashlight, and they carefully climbed a narrow steel staircase with no banisters.

Casey opened Madison's apartment door with his penknife, the only apartment on the second floor, and handed Callahan latex gloves. The apartment had an old dresser and unmade queen-size bed, with dirty sheets, in the bedroom, and a TV and a worn leather couch in the small living room. The shower was as filthy as the rest of the apartment.

"He lives like a tramp. Where does his money go?" Callahan asked.

"Consider the source," Casey said. "We gotta hurry like a house on fire. Let's start in the bedroom. You search his closet. I'll go through his dresser." Callahan pulled out a small cardboard box covered with a gray blanket, putting it on the bed.

Casey opened it. They grew quiet, fixated on the earrings and jewelry taken from Madison's victims, and photos of their tortured, naked bodies. In the bottom of the box was a large envelope. Casey tore it open.

"Take a look," he said, handing it to the priest.

"My God."

Callahan grew dizzy and knelt on the floor.

"Easy does it, Padre."

"I know this woman. Her name is Robin. She used to come to me for help. Madison called himself Rubin Heckler, but it's the same guy. He was her monster boyfriend — he beat her unmercifully, nearly killed her."

The photos showed Robin naked, hands and feet handcuffed to the bedposts, blood dripping out of her mouth and down her legs.

Speechless, Callahan wiped his eyes.

"Christ, we gotta get the hell out of here," Casey said. But as he lifted the box from the bed, the apartment door opened. They both leaped into the back of the closet, clutching the box, barely breathing. Casey pulled out his gun.

They heard Madison go to the refrigerator and pop open a can, then put on his TV; he watched for a while, laughing. They heard him go to the bathroom, groaning in pleasure, and then come into the bedroom. His hands were on the closet doorknob when the phone rang.

"On my way," he said, and rushed out of his apartment.

They slid out of the closet, their clothes drenched in sweat, panting like dogs. Casey grabbed the box. They waited five minutes and then left the warehouse, running to the car.

Casey dropped Callahan off at the rectory. Neither spoke.

"I'll be in touch," Casey said.

Father Callahan didn't answer. He went to his bathroom and heaved his guts out.

CHAPTER 29

Father Callahan's blood pressure spiked when Casey told him that cops would be bringing down Madison that evening.

"This is a covert operation, so there will be no other cops there except Duffy and the three chiefs whose daughters have been murdered. That was their decision. I'll be there, but Duffy is in charge."

"I want to be there," Callahan said. "I have to be there."

"Listen, Padre, I know how you feel, but I don't think it will sit well with the chiefs."

"Just remind Duffy how I helped nail that SOB. You owe me."

"Okay. Okay. I'll get a hold of Duffy — but it's up to him." He began to leave the rectory.

"Call him, here and now."

"Jeez, Padre, calm down."

He went to the phone in the kitchen and dialed. Callahan watched him from the dining room.

Casey hung up and returned to the dining room.

"Good news for you, though I don't know if it will be that good for the rest of us. Chief Duffy agreed, along with a lot of don'ts."

"For instance?"

"You don't leave my side, don't get in the way, don't approach Madison, just be a looker, that's it. Agree?"

"Yes," Callahan said.

"I'll pick you up at six."

"Fine."

* * *

Time dragged until Casey drove up to the rectory in his ratty Ford. No complaints out of Callahan about the rocky seat this time.

At 7 p.m. the four police chiefs and Casey gathered on the first floor inside Madison's warehouse apartment. Chief Duffy spoke.

"I've been informed that Madison has been shopping for groceries. He could be arriving soon."

Casey introduced Father Callahan to the other chiefs, all wearing plain clothes and faces hard as nails. Their handshakes were cold, fast and impatient.

Duffy spoke.

"Keep in mind Madison is a top-grade snake, and with a fifty-fifty chance he'll sniff danger. Be prepared. We'll take him down as soon as he puts his key in his apartment door."

They checked their guns, slid them back into their shoulder holsters. They were all over fifty and a bit bulky, but with a well-muscled fitness that surprised Callahan. And they were angry.

They had parked three unmarked cars two blocks down from the warehouse, but Duffy sat low in a battered Chevy right across from the warehouse, where it fit in nicely with the other dumpy cars on the street.

The three other chiefs took up hidden posts on the second floor, wedged into tight corners. Callahan stayed with Casey on the first floor, shielded by the corner of a hallway. They disconnected all the lights but one to help them hide. Keeping one functional would help offset Madison's suspicions.

Darkness wrapped itself heavily around the buildings and covered the streets. It was a moonless night, and this neighborhood's streetlights had been broken long ago. The only movement seemed to be from cats that had begun to prowl.

A sleek black Cadillac pulled up to the front of the warehouse and a young woman started to step out. Duffy, his hand on his gun, flashed his badge in her face.

"Get the hell out of here," he whispered hoarsely.

Her driver, her pimp, yanked her back into the car. Duffy kicked the door shut and they sped off.

"Christ, what else?" He ran back to his car, sinking so low that his nose rested below the windowsill.

Just minutes later Madison parked in front of the warehouse, got out holding a bag of groceries in each hand, looked from side to side, and moved casually toward the warehouse. Abruptly he stopped. He put down his groceries and lit a cigarette.

Time dragged as he smoked. Tension grew thick. Finally he tossed the butt on the curb, picked up his grocery bags and slowly entered the warehouse. He flipped the wall switch to turn on the lights, noticed that just one worked, and stopped again, looking back and forth.

"Denise, baby, you up there? . . . Fuck you," he said out loud, "always late," then proceeded up the steps.

Callahan crouched next to Casey, his heart pounding and his mind flashing on photos of Robin chained to the bed — and on the photos of the murdered, tortured daughters of these police chiefs.

Madison had just reached the fourth step when Callahan, unable to control his fury, leaped out from behind the corner and tackled him, pushing the killer-rapist-cop-scumbag onto the concrete floor. Before the groceries, flying in all directions, could hit the floor he was on top of Madison, pounding his face and howling in Gaelic like a madman.

Madison, taken completely by surprise, struggled to get a gun from his boot. Casey kicked it out of his hands and grabbed it. The chiefs hurried toward the fight, their guns drawn, stupefied.

"Don't shoot," Duffy yelled. They held back, mesmerized by sight of a priest throwing Madison against the wall, pounding and kicking his body as if he was spearing a bull.

"Maybe we should stop the priest before he kills him," Casey said dryly.

"Let him kill the fuck — it's a matter of self-defense," Duffy replied slowly. The other chiefs moved in closer.

When Madison tried to stand, Callahan kicked his legs out from under him, slamming his head again onto the concrete floor. Finally, Casey ran in and dragged Callahan away. Madison was laid out prostrate, gasping for air.

"Padre, you appear to be a little upset," Casey said.

They cuffed Madison's hands, tied his feet, taped his mouth and dragged him to the entrance of the warehouse.

Duffy drove his car up to the curb and they threw Madison into the back seat. Three cars followed Duffy into the gloom and darkness.

Callahan, still breathing hard, shot his fists into the air.

"Burn in hell," he roared.

The cats and even the rats grew still.

CHAPTER 30

With the greenhouse back in full operation, Bernice organized a
dinner celebration for the volunteers in the church basement. It was
gaily decorated with white, green, and yellow streamers and balloons.
Yellow paper tablecloths, flowered napkins and dainty pots of daisies
graced square tables with seating for four.

The waiters from Best In Town catering service were local
college students doing side jobs to pay for their tuition. The young
men wore white suits and yellow ties, and the women wore short
yellow spring dresses. All kept happy smiles on their faces as they
served food and an abundance of wine.

Callahan sat across from Rosemary, with Derrick on his left and
Bernice on his right.

He rose and tapped his glass, smiling.

"This party is a generous gift from Bernice," gesturing to her, "in
appreciation for your devotion and hard work providing flowers and
food for the poor homebound."

Everyone clapped.

"Enjoy. And if by chance you are too tipsy to drive home, worry
not, cabs will be provided." Everyone clapped again, already giddy
from drink and laughter.

Bernice poured Callahan a glass of nice Barolo wine.

"Drink up," she urged.

"It's been years since I've taken a drink. I fear it will not sit well
with me."

"Oh, come on, a small sip won't hurt."

He complied, and the wine's rich coolness lingered like a lover
on his lips. It was a taste he once craved. In no time, his glass was
refilled.

As the evening drew on, laughter grew louder. The band played rousing versions of "Hot Stuff," and "I'll Be There." The middle of the basement floor was crammed tight with dancers.

Bernice tugged at him playfully. "Come on, dance."

"Another time," he said.

Definitely not with her.

Not that he couldn't. In his youth he had won dance competitions, dancing all the popular Latin and American dances of the time, including Disco and the Hustle, in the nightclubs of Ireland and England. Even as a monk he'd sometimes dance and sing in the monastery's barns, where the horses nickered and perked their ears.

Without warning, Derrick grabbed him and half dragged him to the dance floor.

"Let's see what you can do," Derrick shouted with an evil grin.

The crowd had formed up for a line dance, and the band struck up "Stayin' Alive."

Feeling for once a little relaxed, loose and free, Callahan danced beside Derrick. Everyone clapped, delighted — except Bernice. She watched him, wide-eyed and resentful that he had refused to dance with her.

When he returned to the table she disguised her envy and said mildly, "Where did you learn to dance like that?"

"Most kids dance in Europe," he said nonchalantly, enjoying another sip of wine.

By 11 p.m. everyone had left mellow and happy. The food, tables, kitchen and basement hall were cleaned and Bernice had given generous tips to the caterers, band, and waiters.

Bernice walked him back to the rectory. Lightheaded, he turned to her and said, "That was a great party. Please let yourself out."

Then he walked into his room and collapsed on his bed.

He heard a rustle and opened his eyes to see Bernice slipping out of her dress. Her amazing breasts and firm body moved hypnotically.

His body became excited and he tried to fight it.

"Isn't it hard not having a woman in your bed?" she purred as she moved in next to him.

"I've had my moments," he said, his heartbeat like a freight train.

She pressed her lips —soft, delicious and tantalizing — onto his and moved her hands down to his excited erection. He pulled her body to himself, lost in the moment, starved, wild, kissing her, licking her, frantic to push himself inside her heat.

"Make love to me," she moaned, driving him mad by massaging his large, stiff penis.

He drew his fingers down to the fluid entry of her body and moved on top of her, when someone pounded on the rectory door.

"Don't answer," she begged.

"I must."

With enormous effort, he pulled his body off her and put on his bathrobe, walking barefoot to the front door, opening it.

"Sorry, man," a young man said. "I left my wallet in the kitchen. I was a waiter at your party."

"Come in. I'm sure it's still there."

The young man rushed in, emerged from the kitchen with his wallet and ran off, yelling "Thanks" over his shoulder.

Callahan stood in the kitchen, gulping down a glass of water, running the water full force and slapping it on his face.

"Come back to bed."

He turned to see Bernice's luscious naked body, her hands reaching toward him, longing in her eyes.

"I love you. Come back to bed. Make love to me."

"Please put on your clothes. We need to talk," and he looked at her face steadfastly.

She dressed and came into the living room, where he stood. He spoke slowly, struggling to keep his mind clear.

"This was a mistake. I was half drunk . . . still am. I allowed myself to be put in this situation and that was wrong. You are beautiful, and God knows extremely generous, but I can't be a part of this sexual madness."

She tossed her head back defiantly.

"You've been suffocating your real feelings for me," she cried defiantly. "I know you want to make love to me." Her face flushed with frustration.

"Please understand. The only woman I've ever loved was my wife. I don't love you. I care for you, but not in the way that you want.

And I feel you knew what you were doing, getting me to drink to take advantage of me."

She retorted angrily, and the ugly side of charming Bernice surfaced.

"You're a weak man, a selfish, needy priest," she mocked him.

"I admit to being weak, as a man and as a priest. I'll give you that. But I want to remain celibate, with no woman in my bed — least of all you."

"I hate you! I hate you!" she screamed, throwing her purse against the living room wall, its contents flying in every direction. He waited, ignoring her tantrum.

"I have no problem with hate, but you've created a trinity of illusionary love, sex and hate, and have blamed it on me."

His anger grew as she gathered her purse's contents from the floor.

She tossed her lipstick, handkerchiefs, wallet and car keys into her purse.

"Help me put on my coat."

He kept his distance and asked, his voice hard, "Did you arrange this celebration with the purpose of seducing me?"

No response. In a measured tone he said, "Given this distressing situation, I don't want you to return to this parish. Your presence here has become a sickness for both of us. Say all your good-byes to the greenhouse volunteers tomorrow. You are replaceable — though no one will equal you," he added softly.

She quieted, shocked and silent. Through tears she said, "I admit to taking shameless advantage of you. And I lost my temper. Tomorrow will be my last day with the greenhouse volunteers."

"I wish you every happiness," he said sadly.

She threw open the rectory door, leaving it wide open, ran to her new Bentley and raced off into the thick fog.

* * *

As the sun rose he drove to the monastery in the Catskills, depressed in mind, body and spirit. Half a mile from the monastery he stopped at a viewing spot, got out and drew in the freshness of spring air that was shedding the weary skin of winter. Birds flew about, chattering exuberantly as they prepared for new life.

Despair, frustration, anger and self-loathing filled his heart and mind as he fought to rid himself of his sexual experience with Bernice. He squatted low on his haunches on the viewing platform at the cliff's edge, closing his eyes.

A punishing voice inside his mind taunted, *You are unworthy to be a monk or a priest. You are a hypocrite, worst of the worst, preaching aberrance to God's commandments*. The caustic voice continued drumming inside his head until he became dizzy and slipped onto the ground at the edge of the cliff, a drop of five thousand feet.

Disoriented, he felt himself being lifted like a feather back toward his car.

"Blessings be upon you, my son."

He looked up into the radiant countenance of Monk Thron, who was leaning against his car.

"I could have fallen to my death," Callahan gasped as he rubbed his eyes. "I felt myself slipping but I had no strength to stop."

"It is not your destiny to go flying through the air, like some superman," the monk said, chuckling.

"How did you know that I was in trouble, that I needed help?"

"Your soul called to me," the monk said simply with a slight bow.

Again, Callahan accepted that the little monk seemed to live in a mystical world that made no reasonable sense.

When they arrived at the monastery the bells tolled, inviting peace and tranquility. The scent of lilacs greeted them as Monk Thron led him to a guest cottage with a single bed, a small dresser, a tiny bathroom and large windows that provided a view to a mountain of trees. The pungent scent of white lilies filled the room.

He put his duffel bag on the floor and followed the monk to a plain dining room with white walls and pine chairs and tables. A young monk with shaved head served them tea and crumpets on small white plates. They ate in silence, and Callahan began to feel his mind enter calmness.

When they had finished, Monk Thron rose.

"Please take off your shoes," and he did. "I want you to feel the sacred earth beneath your feet, and listen to nature's mysteries while we walk. It will open your heart in peace."

"Peace? I fear I will never experience a whisper of peace again."
The monk smiled.

"What you fear, my son, shall pass — as all things do."

They moved through the winding paths of the woods, greeted by rabbits and chipmunks.

"I have sinned grievously," Callahan said, casting his eyes down, unable to look the holy monk in the face. Thron remained silent and moved steadily into the soul of the forest.

In time the monk stopped, laid a white blanket on the ground, gestured to Callahan to rest and gave him water from his small jug. Together they closed their eyes, crossing their legs in a restful position.

"I am suffering," Callahan said, revealing his turbulent experience with Bernice. "I wanted the sex, but I don't love that woman. Maybe I could learn to love her. Maybe we could be secret lovers." His voice broke like glass. "It's insane. It's torturous. I don't want any of that."

Monk Thron listened.

"My son, through pain and suffering we learn compassion. For most of humanity it is the best way. The popular phrase is 'to hang in there.'"

Father Callahan smiled at the slang.

"Is there no other way?"

"Most definitely . . . but only for the dead," and the little monk shook with laughter. "The healing of time is our most precious gift."

Once more they embraced the grace of silence until Callahan spoke.

"I told Bernice to cease working at the church and not to return. But I feel guilty. She's done so much, and she's been so generous."

"Ah, the ugly snake of guilt raises its head again. You spoke from a position of truth and strength. This woman knows you did the right thing, and in her heart she most certainly knows she did the wrong thing.

"Let us return to the monastery. By remaining overnight, your body, mind and spirit will be refreshed and healed, my son."

As they entered the serenity of the monastery he felt a welcome lightness of being. He was no longer consumed by a sense of sinfulness.

When he returned to the rectory the next day, Rosemary greeted him.

"I'll miss Bernice. She dropped this note off this morning and asked me to give it to you. Said she's moving to Aspen, Colorado, to live near her sister's family.

He opened a perfumed note.

Please forgive me for my behavior.

Bernice

Enclosed was a check for fifty thousand dollars. He tore both the note and the check into tiny pieces and tossed them into the trash.

CHAPTER 31

He opened the New York Times to the Arts section, which featured a full-page article and photos of the world-renowned sculptor Pete O'Connor. In the largest photo, O'Connor was standing beside a magnificent marble sculpture of a green dragon, six feet tall, that was on display at the Metropolitan Museum of Art. The article noted that the artist would be attending a public reception at 6 p.m. that Saturday.

In his wildest dreams he could not believe that Pete O'Connor would be in New York City —with a sculpture of a dragon, no less. It had been many years since he had tattooed the Celtic dragon on Callahan's back.

On Saturday, a cab dropped him off in front of the old museum's imposing building at the eastern edge of Central Park. Throngs of people, young and old, moved quickly through its front doors. He squeezed in among the crowd, in his priest's black suit and white collar. Excitement was too small a word for the way he felt, hoping to meet the fiery Pete O'Connor again.

A mature, stately woman waved the visitors into an enormous room where walls displayed O'Connor's paintings of women, children, and Ireland's beautiful landscapes. In the center of the room, soft light illuminated the glorious Irish-emerald marble dragon. A red rope circled the sculpture, protecting it from unclean hands.

People's chatter fell to a sacred hush at the sight of the magnificent dragon, seeming so lifelike at six feet tall. The mother dragon's outstretched wings caressed her male offspring, snuggled tightly to her rounded belly. Its small face gazed into its mother's jet-black eyes. Her long beak rested gently, carefully, on his small shoulder. At the base of the statue, in gold, was a single word: Love.

Callahan stood reverently in front of the sculpture, transfixed by its spectacular beauty. In the far corner, O'Connor was engaged in lively conversation, surrounded by admirers and signing autographs.

Yet the artist kept an eye on all those beholding his masterpiece, and he drew back in surprise when he saw John Callahan, no longer a wild hooligan on Belfast's streets, but a grown man — and a priest?

He hurried to his side.

"'Tis a fine day indeed to see the likes of you, a far cry from years gone by," O'Connor said with a lilting laugh.

Callahan swung around and hugged him impulsively.

"Dare I ask if that dragon tattoo remains on your back?" and the question danced in his eyes.

"Yes, and it shall remain until my body dries up. But I thought you hated dragons. When I was a lad, you called them breasts devoid of heart and soul."

"Ah, so I did. Come closer," the artist whispered as he pulled the priest away from the crowd.

"I kept that sketch of your tattoo in my back room. Hidden. I'd glance at it once in a while. But in time this dragon sketch demanded to be seen, so I put it in on my desk in the front of the studio. In spite of myself, I began talking to it as if it was real. Strange, eh?"

"Not so strange," Callahan said, having experienced too much of the strange during the past ten months.

"Two years past, a good friend and benefactor gave me this large piece of emerald marble for my birthday."

O'Connor glanced around, satisfied that no one was eavesdropping.

"On that same day when I was airing out my studio a wind rushed in, from God knows where, and tossed all my papers every which way.

"I shut all the windows and the door and started to pick up the mess. That's when I found your dragon tattoo sketch stuck hard on that marble. I pulled it off, but I thought my mind had left me."

"Understandable," Callahan said more loudly, as the noise of excitement in the museum had grown.

"For the rest of the week I kept running my hands over this marble, deliciously smooth to my touch. I'd take the sketch from time to time and place it against it. I felt as happy as a little kid whenever I did that."

Then O'Connor swept his hands through the air toward the dragon.

"She became my passion, and 'tis you I owe."

"And I owe you as well," Callahan said.

"I declare on God's holy earth . . . hard to believe . . . you a priest."

"Often I can't believe it myself," Callahan said, grinning.

"Where do you live?"

"Here in New York City. Please, take my card. Come visit me."

"I wish . . . but I need to be back in Dublin tomorrow, please God. And New York City still gives me the scares; wild traffic, harried people rushing hither and yon."

"I've gotten rather used to it, though I thought I never would. In fact, I have come to enjoy the foghorns bellowing off the Hudson."

"Will you come back to Ireland?" Pete asked.

"The future is not mine to know, Callahan answered. "But I have discovered that here," as he touched his heart," I am at home among sinners."

O'Connor pulled back the ropes protecting the dragon.

"You may touch her."

Then he watched Callahan caress the baby dragon and its mother's adoring face, as one would a lover. The priest was lost in the simple joy of touching them as if they were real creatures.

In moments, a four-year-old boy tugged at Callahan's trousers, shrieking, "Baby drag — . . . drag — " with his little arms stretched toward the statue.

Callahan picked up the child and took him to the sculpture, where the boy threw his little arms around the dragon's baby.

Applause and laughter filled the room as everyone embraced the magic of the moment.

With that, O'Connor quickly removed the ropes and every child in the room ran up to the dragon, shrieking with pleasure, rubbing and kissing it.

Then the artist rushed to get a sketchpad.

* * *

Four weeks had passed and all was peaceful at Saint Francis of Assisi Church on a Saturday afternoon. Groups of children had left the greenhouse after learning to cultivate the flowers under the careful supervision of Charles Robins, a volunteer who had replaced Bernice as the greenhouse manager.

Casey watched them leave as he entered the rectory, then sat comfortably beside Callahan at the dining table to enjoy a large slice of pizza and a Coke.

"Must say, you look rather sporty with that deep tan of yours. The Bahamas must have agreed with you."

"My vacation was the best in my life," Casey said, loudly biting into the crust of his pizza.

"That good?"

"Yep, plenty of yummy, spicy food, great surfing . . . pretty women loving me." He was in high spirits.

"It looks like they had a ton to love," Callahan said, snickering at the detective's weight gain.

"Come on, Padre, no one was complaining."

"Casey, whatever happened to that cockroach Madison? Is he in solitary at Riker's Island?"

Casey rocked back in his chair, pretending to be thoughtful.

"Madison was taken to parts unknown."

"What do you mean, to parts unknown?"

"Just to be brief, I'll put it this way. Madison has a new address, residing somewhere cold and deep in the Atlantic."

Both men roared, and the subject was dropped. Callahan knew that a priest should say a prayer for Madison's soul, but he couldn't. He would resolve that conflicted feeling some other time.

"Where's Rosemary?" Casey asked, now into his second piece of pizza and licking his fingers.

"She's visiting relatives for a few days."

"I noticed she's been looking much happier since Alex's been gone," Casey said.

"He died recently at Saint Michael's Retirement Center, just after I visited him. Alex was a changed man, and we got on quite well."

"Jeez, lots going on since I've been on holiday."

Casey flashed on Bernice for a brief second, but let it rest.

"What's with all those kids running down the street from the greenhouse?"

"They love planting and working with the flowers, thanks to Charles. He's doing a fine job."

"Must be great having kids around here," Casey said.

"It's the best thing going on around here," Callahan replied.

"Truth be told, Padre, I thought you'd be back in the lush moors of Ireland by now, chanting with those sanctified monks, away from New York City's sin, crime, and dirt," he said, rolling his eyeballs.

"Actually, I have been invited to perform a marriage ceremony for Sheila, a former parishioner who has moved to Tuscany. I'm still considering it."

"Ponder no longer, Padre. Just go — cut loose — have fun," Casey urged him with a mischievous wink.

* * *

An hour after Casey had left, a small truck drove into the rectory's driveway. Two men carried out a wooden crate and rang the bell.

"We have a package for a Father John Callahan," the taller man said. "May we come in?" and handed him an envelope edged in gold leaf.

It gave me enormous pleasure after so many long years to have been with you.

Enjoy,
Pete O'Connor.

"We were given instructions to put this painting wherever you desire."

"Take it to my bedroom," Callahan said, opening the door.

They proceeded carefully, removing the nails and wood from the crate. They pulled out a five-by-five-foot oil painting covered with a thin brown paper. He pointed to the large back wall in his bedroom, and they hung it with care and left.

He removed the paper from the painting slowly, amazed, staring at a figure of a tall, muscular man, naked to his waist. The sun's flaming colors of scarlet and gold were set against a brilliant aqua sky. The man's arms reached toward the Irish Sea and his bare feet were planted deep in the moor's rugged soil.

On the man's back was an emerald dragon, with her large-veined wings covering him protectively. Her sharp, bony head was turned and her ebony eyes watchful, with her powerful legs curled around him.

Callahan's heart pounded as he studied the dragon's wings. Very tiny feathers, easily missed, grew from her wings and the top of her head, and around her clawed feet.

He remembered O'Connor's words from years past. "As a boy you will see what you are prepared to see and know, and when you become a man you will see far more and know much more."

He smiled as he moved his fingers prayerfully over the gold-edged letters on the bottom of the frame:

PROTECT AND DEFEND

Join the Conversation!

Learn more about Author Elizabeth Upton on the Web!

www.elizabethaupton.com

And join us on Facebook at . . .

http://facebook.com/elizabethaupton